GRANT'S
flame

SHARK'S EDGE: BOOK FIVE

ANGEL PAYNE & VICTORIA BLUE

GRANT'S
flame

SHARK'S EDGE: BOOK FIVE

ANGEL PAYNE & VICTORIA BLUE

WATERHOUSE PRESS

*For David, Ivy, and Kadin. Thank you for proving
to me how bright this family's flame can glow.*

I love you all so dearly.

—XO VB

For you, man of my life and mate of my soul:

Thomas, you are my everything.

—Angel

CHAPTER ONE

GRANT

Watching over Rio while she slept calmed my nerves. She was a respite for my weary soul, which was ironic, really, because I'd been alternating between pacing around the stateroom, feverishly checking my phone for on the fire at Clear Horizons, the mental health facility I'd sprung her from the afternoon prior, and joining her. Molding my body against hers on the large bed that occupied about half the room was a balm for my invisible wounds, and my God, a spoonful of sugar really did help the medicine go down.

My normally restless little nymph had been sleeping for close to fifteen hours. Even now, as I pulled her close and gently kissed her nape, she barely stirred. Whatever sedative the hospital staff had given her had really knocked her on her ass. Other than a couple of bathroom visits throughout the night, the woman had slept more since we'd cast off from the dock in Los Angeles than I'd seen her tally in the past month.

The observation both comforted and alarmed me. On one hand, I was happy that our floating haven of tranquility was an ease to her jumbled mind and not another agitation. But that was where my comfort stopped, and I became a worse basket case by the hour. Was she sleeping too long? Was this normal, or was there something else wrong—something I needed to be concerned about? Should I wake her and insist she eat? When had she'd last eaten? And by that, I meant actual food. When she worked at Abstract, she often denied herself anything until after the lunch deliveries, despite being surrounded by nourishing options. Even then, she usually scarfed a protein bar or some equally inadequate meal substitute while she drove.

It was settled. She needed to eat, and this time, I was positive about the decision. So, with a steadying inhale, I gently curved a hand over the ball of her shoulder and prepared to wake her. But just like last time—and each of the times before that—I quickly pulled my hand back, second-guessing the resolution.

Fuck.

It was the act—well, the non-act—of a coward. I knew that, damn it. But it changed nothing. The second I thought about waking her, my mind instantly went down a complicated, thorny path—right to the conversation we would need to have when I did so. No matter what kind of verbal clover we planted to make the subject prettier, it would be a bramble-covered mess underneath.

We had to talk about the clusterfuck I'd pulled her from yesterday.

All of it.

Even if all the brambles poked back out again, re-exposing the truth. Because sometimes the truth was just the ugly, unavoidable truth. It was burning and irritating and aggravating and downright awful, no matter how many ways we danced around it. And the persistent resin of this particular topic would stay around long after its source was gone.

I huffed loudly and scrubbed a hand down my unshaven

face and continued the movement until I gripped my tense and knotted neck.

My movements caused Rio to turn over and open her groggy eyes. It took her a few moments to focus in my direction, then around the cabin, silently taking in her surroundings. At least she didn't bolt from the bed. That was a win I would greedily count.

"Where are we?"

A beat of silence went by, mandated solely by my selfishness. Her voice, husky from so much slumber, made me think of sexy love songs. The typical whiskey hue of her irises had gone dark and glassy from the medication she'd been given. She seemed challenged by maintaining a fixed gaze on a singular point. But according to the abundant—okay, obsessive—research I'd gotten in while she slept, all these conditions were completely normal, considering what she'd been through.

Riiiggghhttt. Normal.

I just had to keep reminding myself of that.

"Are you thirsty, baby?" The term of endearment slipped back into place so easily, and I inwardly chastised myself. I had no idea where things stood between us now, but the last thing I wanted to do was spook her or distract her with an innocent tangent at the moment.

Move on. I had to simply move on.

The purpose got me to my feet again. With a determined stride, I moved to the nightstand. A tray with a hand-painted terra-cotta ewer of ice water and several glasses sat in invitation. One of the galley crew members had artfully wrapped a white linen napkin around the jug, absorbing the condensation that formed on the exterior, even though the stateroom was air-conditioned. I poured her a glass about half full and then returned, nudging a spot on the bed near her hip so she'd make room for me to sit beside her.

"Thank you," she said once I'd settled.

"Of course," I responded good-naturedly and urged the glass at her.

She sat up fully and scooted back against the upholstered headboard. I made a fuss trying to prop pillows all around so she was encased in a down and feather nest. The yacht, which I'd researched for weeks in my hope to get Rio out of LA for a while, was elegantly appointed with all the comforts of a luxurious hotel. Included in my booking, which they'd luckily been able to accommodate last minute, was a small crew experienced in every aspect of personal service. They were here to fulfill our every whim and desire but give us complete privacy while doing so.

Rio looked around the room again, brow furrowed with a heavy crease. "Where did you say we were again?" she asked, but I couldn't be sure how much she was ready to hear.

As I sat on the bed, I watched her carefully. The distance between us seemed safe. Friendly but not aloof. "Are you afraid of open water?" I asked gently, reaching out to stroke her leg and then pulling back at the last moment when I realized what I was about to do.

"As opposed to what?" she returned. "Closed water?"

I let her new crack go by. I had to stick to the subject. "As in the ocean, compared to a lake or river."

"No, of course not. I grew up near Baltimore, as you know. I was practically raised on the Chesapeake Bay. In Seal Beach, I'm a block from the Pacific. Remember?"

I paused, consciously holding back the first answer that

came to mind. I'd been forcing myself *not* to remember her little cottage in Seal Beach. One, because it was the house she bought and shared with her late husband, who was killed on a construction site for my best friend's company. Two, because it was the place yours truly first got naked and horizontal with her. Forgetting both those facts was as hard as one might imagine—just for very divergent reasons.

"Yeah," I finally stammered. "Of course. Right. Well, that's good. Really good."

Her dark brows pulled together. "Why?"

"Because we're cruising on the Pacific Ocean," I answered, taking the now-empty glass from her. "And will be for a few days. Honolulu is our destination."

Good thing I'd gotten the glass back when I did. Within half a second, Rio jerked higher and looked around the room again. "Okay, back up the wagon."

"Well, technically it's a yacht."

"What did you just say?" she plowed on, prompting my own small scowl. I wasn't sure which detail was hanging her up.

I scooted back a little farther, occupying the space next to her calf now. The whole time, I watched her carefully. Her composure was still notably cautious. I related, though I hid it better.

"What's wrong?" I asked gently. "What has you worried?"

"Really? This is a boat?" She swung her head back and forth, dark bedhead hair not moving from where it was stubbornly matted down from heavy sleep. "It's nicer than my house, for God's sake."

I looked around the room again, trying to see things through her eyes. It definitely was a well-appointed vessel.

"Well, it's a different kind of beautiful than your place, but I'm glad you like it." I tried to infuse my words with the right amount of excitement. "Wait. You do like it, right?"

When Rio reached out far enough to clutch my fingertips with her own, my heart skipped a couple of beats. Seriously, like I was sixteen years old again. This woman—this fucking gorgeous woman—and her hold over me . . .

"I like it a lot," she husked. "And thank you." She looked down and picked nervously at the blanket. "I'm just not used to surroundings like this."

"You're going to love the rest of it, then, too. Do you want to get up and walk around? Might be nice to go up top and see the sunshine and ocean." I stiffened though, worrying again about her unknown fears. The freak-out I'd witnessed in her private room at Clear Horizons would stay with me for life. I'd walk barefoot over hot coals before subjecting her to those kinds of emotions again.

"What is it?" This time she was the one to ask, tilting her head like a curious puppy. "You just got very worried about something." She physically twitched, as though an answer balloon just popped right over her head. "Oh, Grant, this isn't Sebastian's boat, is it?"

She started pushing the covers down her thighs, until realizing she was only wearing one of my T-shirts, and then quickly pulled them back up.

The alarm that one thought conjured, however, never left her face. "He's not here, is he?" Her voice rose with the same level of distress her movements had. Each word tumbled out atop the next, making it close to impossible to understand what she was asking.

"No," I reassured her gently, but her eyes shot around the

room as though she still expected my best friend to spring from one of the closets and yell *Surprise!*

"No." My repetition was sterner. I dropped my voice by an octave, compelling her to re-center on me. Oh, hell yes. Just the way I liked it. Exactly the way I liked her.

I slid my hand over and placed my open palm on her blanket-covered leg. But the moment we both gazed at where our hands rested, I pulled back just as quickly as before.

You don't get to do that, man.

I frowned. God, I wasn't used to this kind of awkwardness. This sense of not knowing where I stood with a woman. The feeling was damned unsettling. "Sebastian doesn't have anything to do with this," I said with quiet reassurance. "I chartered this boat. For you. For us."

"You did?" she asked, bewildered. After scrunching her forehead and looking around the stateroom again, she said, "But . . . why?"

I shrugged. "Seemed like a good idea. I don't know, the right thing to do. Clearly you needed to get out of Los Angeles for a little while."

I raised my gaze to meet hers head-on. Time to get really serious—and really honest. "Away from all the things that were pulling you under."

She grinned and rubbed the top of her head, making her hair stick up like a baby bird's new downy feathers. "Is that what you think was happening?"

"What?" I was more taken aback by her mischievous grin than her mocking tone. Unfortunately, I'd grown far too used to her sarcasm for that part to bother me. But her open amusement? That was new. And troubling.

When was I going to figure this woman out? And why did I keep trying?

Time for another tactic. "Let's get some food in you." I stood to get my cell phone off the table. "I'll feel so much better if you eat something."

"Isn't that backwards?" she volleyed back, looking up at me with large, challenging eyes.

"For fuck's sake, woman," I answered in a rush of frustration. "Is it so hard to comprehend I've been worried about you?"

She continued her wordless glare.

"Is this what happens when you finally get some sleep? Everything becomes a damn battle?"

"I just thought it was funny. Normally people say, 'You'll feel better if you eat.' But you said you'll feel better if I eat." She gave a careless shrug. "I don't know, it just sounded backwards. You managed to make my eating about you." She looked down to fiddle with the comforter that was tucked neatly around her legs.

Finally thinking a redirect was best, I said, "I'll go get you something to eat." I backed toward the door, thumbing over my shoulder to indicate the exit. "If you feel like a shower, there's a fully stocked bathroom here." I tapped on the door that led into the stateroom's private head. "And there are some clothes that should fit you in . . . the . . . closet . . ."

I let my words trail off as her face twisted with discomfort. The look was stealing the damn oxygen from my lungs.

"Blaze, what is it?"

Are you cold? I'll keep you warm. Scared? I'll protect you. Lonely? I'll hold you. Tell me, it's yours. I'm yours.

"Did I have things . . ." She gave her head a little shake.

I waited a few beats, but she didn't finish. "What is it? Ask me, baby," I issued resolutely after watching her struggle with even the simplest question. "I'll give you whatever truth I can, I promise."

"Did I have personal things when you came for me?" She finally lifted her eyes to meet mine. "At the hospital? Or whatever that place was?" She swallowed so roughly after asking the question, I could see her throat process the entire movement from where I stood across the room.

My voice came out quieter than I expected. "I can't be sure. If you did, they didn't make it out with us. I just grabbed you, and we left. There wasn't much time to think things through. I mean, with the fire, and . . . you . . ." I drifted off, leaving that subject to dangle in the all-too-quiet room. I was pretty sure neither of us was ready to have that conversation anyway. "But Reina, saint that she is, was able to bring some things for you before the boat left LA . . . so . . ." I awkwardly thumbed toward the bathroom again.

Jesus Christ, when did everything become so uncomfortable between us? I needed to get the hell out of this room, though, and breathe for a minute, so I powered through the last bit. "Why don't you get a shower, and then we can talk more over breakfast? We have nothing but time now."

"Uhh . . . okay." She gave a little nod, and I was out the door without another word.

The two laps I took around the outside deck were exactly what I needed to get my head back in the game. Except when I got back to the stateroom about twenty minutes later, Rio was in the exact same spot in which I'd left her. The faraway look had returned to her face, and she visibly startled when I opened the door.

"That was fast," she muttered, looking at me after a few beats.

"We're not on a schedule. At all. If you want to sit right there in that same spot for three days, then that's what you should do. I just need you to eat and drink and sleep. Would I love for you to go outside and see the sun while it's up? Maybe let the fresh air blow over your skin?" I nodded soundly. "But I won't force you to do anything."

While I spoke, she kept staring at me with her wide chocolate eyes. They were always so much darker while we were indoors, I noticed. Outside, especially in the SoCal weather, her irises picked up the golden flecks of the sun, and her big baby doll expressions lit up more like liquid amber then. But in either setting, in any place, noticing things about her—noticing everything about her—had become my favorite pastime. Since meeting her, my world had become a brighter, bolder adventure. Even now.

Suddenly, she kicked back the covers. Before I could figure out what she was doing, she shot up from the bed. Immediately, she swayed on her feet. "Whoa," she groaned and plopped back down on the mattress. "Oh, holy shit. Stop the world. I want to get off." She squeezed her eyes shut while a low moan escaped her lips and then gripped both sides of her head as if she could steady the spinning from holding on to the outside.

"Maybe you should get some food in you first and shower after?" I offered, already feeling pathetically helpless again. "I have no idea when you ate last. They should be almost done with setting up breakfast right now." Though my phrasing was suggestive and open, no way I was letting her slide on getting some nutrition. Her bout of dizziness had sealed the deal on my determination.

"Grant."

Her tone was impatient, but two could play at that

imperious-and-not-budging game. "Yes?"

We both just stared at one another. This woman and her feisty will made my balls ache in a way they shouldn't, but some things would never change, I guessed.

And did I really want them to?

Finally realizing she wasn't going to win this standoff, she let her hands flop to her sides on the mattress. "Look." She sighed. "You don't have to wait on me like this."

"No waiting going on here," I defended evenly. "All I'm doing is just seeing to your well-being. And now you can't even argue that you're not hungry. You're going to pass out soon if you don't eat something. Now come on." I held my arm out like a gentlemanly escort. "I'll make sure you don't faceplant along the way."

She ducked in front of the oval mirror that hung above the dresser. "But I can't go anywhere looking like this." She winced while finger-combing her bangs into some sort of order.

"There's no one on the entire boat but the crew and us. But you won't even see them unless you want to. They've all been specifically instructed and well paid to ensure it. Come." I motioned again with my outstretched arm.

"Don't call to me like I'm your pet."

A growl of frustration slipped out, and I wasn't sure I regretted it. "Stop trying to pick a fight at every turn. You need nourishment. Your attitude is atrocious. And if food doesn't work, we can talk about other ways to clean it up."

I raised my brows while I waited for her come back. I knew I was poking the little beast now, but she was too tempting in her sour mood. I was willing to overlook a few things about her snippiness—to a point. Because I really wanted to take her over my knee and get it over with. I had to keep remembering she'd been through hell and back in the past few weeks. Still, the whole production was starting to get out of hand, and I had a feeling she was pushing my buttons on purpose. She and I had been on this merry-go-round before, after all.

"You can stow the bossy shit, Mr. Twombley," she finally said, turning to face me. Her hair continued to be the same frightful mess, and the corner of her eyes were bracketed in weariness. "Lead the way. I'm fine to walk on my own, though, thank you." She looked at my offered arm sourly and then up to my face to find me examining her.

Shit. I hoped this trip was the right call. Cracks were forming in this beautiful creature's soul right before my very eyes, and I had to find a way to fix them. Because that's what I did. I was the guy who fixed things for people. But never—and I really meant ever—had the mission been more vital than with this woman. I couldn't screw this one up.

"What?" she snapped.

"Nothing, Blaze." When she got within arm's length, I pulled her into my body, whether she wanted to reciprocate my embrace or not. Her arms hung limply at her sides while I circled mine around her shoulders and kissed the top of her head. She didn't push away, as I'd been anticipating. Instead, she sagged completely against me. And goddamn, did it feel amazing. Her nearness. Her trust.

Her heat . . .

No. Not there.

I was in Gentleman Grant mode. I had to keep remembering that. Even if it killed me. And it just might.

"I've missed you," I confessed into her tangled hair. "All of you. Your sassy mouth, your bad attitude, and even your rude eye rolls. I'm glad we're doing this."

I pecked her forehead while she stared up at me, parting her mouth on a bit of bewilderment. At least that was what I hoped for. Confusion I could work with. So much better than punchy temper.

Yeah, this was going to be an interesting journey, all right. But first steps first. Rio needed food and sunshine. I was hoping a fat dose of both would put me fully back on the right side of this woman's good graces. I wanted to help her heal, inside and out.

Because I cared so much about her, and I cared a hell of a lot about us, whatever that shaped up to look like now.

CHAPTER TWO

RIO

Go away. Go away. Go away.

Didn't seem to matter how many times I inwardly repeated the command. Those damn tingles dancing across my skin wouldn't stop their passionate little cha-cha, no matter how fierce my demands were.

Freaking Grant Twombley. The man with his sexy grin and rumbly chuckle . . . and confident embrace . . . that I wished would never end. He had a way of stirring feelings that could be felt all the way down in my toes as he held me against his firm—and damn it, I meant firm—body.

Just from a damn hug!

But it wasn't just a hug. It was everything he'd done for me. Everything he'd dropped in his life, without a thought, to be there for me. Everything he was still doing for me. Because, unlike almost everyone else in my life, he thought I was worth it. And I swore to God, for a fraction of a second, he had me believing it too. The feeling—true self-esteem, and not the act I had everyone believing on a day-to-day basis—made the tingles better and worse at the same time.

The swimming fog in my brain wasn't helping matters currently, but that was definitely there before he pulled me close for this unrequited hug. I needed food. Yep. I was sticking to that story.

"Well, let me go so we can do this, then." My words were muffled against his shirt that smelled of his intoxicating signature Bleu.

Finally, he backed away. I hurried past, easily ducking under his outstretched arm that held the cabin door so it wouldn't slam shut behind me. I stood to the side and allowed Grant to take the lead, quietly falling into step behind him since I didn't know the way.

The boat was extraordinary. Everywhere I looked, luxurious furnishings were trimmed with decadent touches. Fixtures were polished to perfection. Artwork hung on the walls and looked like original work—not mass-market prints. Even the carpet here in the hall and main living spaces was as plush as it was in our private cabin.

I had to admit, only to myself of course, that if a girl had to be suddenly whisked away, this was a mighty fine way to do it.

"I had them set up breakfast on the aft deck," Grant declared. "I think a little fresh air will do you some good."

But when he slowed and turned to make sure I was still in tow, I caught a hint of nervousness in his normally confident expression.

A very unusual countenance for the man I knew.

And cared for. Deeply.

"What's up, big guy? Can't swim? Maybe they have some water wings you can wear while we're on deck," I teased.

He squinted his eyes playfully but didn't hold the expression longer than a few seconds before sobering. "Very funny, brat. I'm more worried about your reaction."

I cocked my head. "Why?"

"Because I care about you. I want you to be comfortable, Rio."

I stepped over and wrapped a hand around his forearm. He was nothing but corded muscle there, but it wasn't enough to cover his continuing concern. For me. For what I thought.

All of that should have freaked me out all over again . . . but it didn't. I knew how the man felt about me. And just because I hadn't made peace with my feelings for him yet didn't mean they weren't there.

But right now, as we stepped through a tinted sliding glass door and out onto the deck, I vowed to be okay with everything about this moment. Because maybe he was right. Maybe this was exactly what I needed.

Warm, salty air filled my lungs, immediately lightening my mood even more. It was a Pavlovian reaction to living in seaside towns the majority of my life. The briny scent of ocean air and the sounds of the water lapping against the transom immediately filled me with a sense of peace and familiarity.

A steward came over to speak quietly to Grant, who in turn looked back to me. "Blaze? Sun or shade?" He motioned to where the table was set up, currently in the full rays of the morning sun.

"That's fine," I returned with a small smile. "Just leave it where it is."

"I don't want you to get burned. You're so pasty."

"I'm not pasty," I protested. "Rude."

"Mmm, okay." He let the lazy grin spread across his lips before turning back to the crewman and asked, "Can you bring up some sun block for Ms. Gibson, please? Thank you."

When he turned back to find me glaring in his direction, hands planted firmly on hips, he laughed.

"What? You seriously don't want a sunburn on our first day, do you? It will ruin days of adventure."

"Days, huh?"

Days, he mouthed, no real sound coming out.

I just shook my head at his nonsense, but I could feel my smile betraying me, and damn it, it actually felt good.

"Come"—he patted the chair—"sit and eat." My charming companion took up a dutiful stance behind the thing, waiting for me to be seated so he could push me in closer to the table. Once I was settled, he took the chair to my right. I watched, quietly amused and charmed, while he moved the place setting from across the table to the position where he sat instead.

"Why do you always do that?" I wondered aloud.

"Hmmm? Do what?"

"Why do you always sit beside me instead of across from me?"

He was about to pull down his sunglasses from their nest in his thick blond waves but paused to observe me with the full capability of his knowing blues. "I like to be close to you, Rio. But if it bothers you, I can move back."

"No." I caught him again by the forearm, preventing him from gesturing to the original seat. "Please no." But touching him was going to become a bad habit if I didn't curb my heated urges, so I whipped back my hand like I'd touched a hot plate. "Just . . . leave it be for now. After that whole production you just went through, it'll be lunch before we get food in our stomachs."

For a long second, he didn't move. Holy Christ, his gaze nearly matched the gleaming waves for intensity. "Rio?"

"What?" I snapped.

"You seem agitated, baby."

"I'm not agitated."

"Do you want to sit inside instead? Maybe the sun is too

much with whatever medication they—"

"No! And I'm not agitated!" As soon as I shouted it, I huffed and hauled in an exaggerated breath.

Okay, so that wasn't very convincing. But I gave myself a silent back pat for the effort plus a giant dose of self-forgiveness. I was one big exposed nerve right now, justifiably so.

I dropped my face into my hands and rested back into the soft chair cushion. Oh shit, the thing was comfortable. Its high padded back and big cushy arms seemed to swallow me up like a small child. So far, this was my favorite part of Grant's little adventure. This would make a great cuddling and reading spot for Robert and me.

Oh no.

I repeated it in a shriek while jolting to my feet, making my chair teeter on its back two legs. The heft of the thing made it land back solidly. My mind and heart weren't so lucky.

"Ohhh, no no no!"

"Rio?"

"Oh, Grant! Oh my God!"

"Rio? Hey." Slowly, he stood too. For some reason, his height seemed even more imposing when he unfolded with such measured wariness. "Blaze, what's—"

I grabbed for his hand, knocking over a water glass and drenching his carefully aligned silverware and plate. "We have to go back! Please, right now! We have to turn the boat around and go back!"

He didn't budge. With maddening silence, he just kept staring cautiously at my hysterics.

In mounting fear and frustration, I tugged on his sleeve. I'd rip the whole thing off his arm if I had to. But I didn't. Instead, I began pacing back and forth, wringing my hands, taking about four long strides before pivoting and starting over again. The motion didn't help. If anything, the adrenaline just jacked my agitation and sorrow.

"How could I be so irresponsible?" I muttered to myself. "How?"

"Damn it, Rio. What's going on?" Grant tried to intercept my pacing, but I turned and headed the other way.

"I'm the absolute worst human on this planet." I tugged on my hair until my scalp stung, fighting to ground myself before my anxiety spun out of control.

Too late, sister!

The self-recrimination was here now. Front and center in my senses—which scrambled and raced, desperately wondering if I could sneak off and even ignite a few matches without being noticed. That wouldn't hurt anyone, right? Wasn't like I wanted to torch the whole boat or anything...

Not. Happening. At least not now. Damn it!

So my panic climbed. "No wonder everyone leaves me," I sobbed out, turning on my heel at the end of my little circuit. "I mean, no wonder, right?"

"Blaze." He tried to stop me again. And again, I beelined right around him.

"I can't believe I would even consider—"

"Enough!"

He thundered the decree against my back. At the same time, he snaked his long arm around my front, securing my body back against his. Sly, sneaky bastard. He approached from behind, making it impossible to dodge him. His hold was ruthless, and his enforcing growl was threaded with raw command.

To my shock, both were exactly what I needed.

I didn't stop to question why. I only knew that I could take a full breath again. That this captivity was suddenly my safe security. That he'd made my maniacal ranting stop, so I'd give him my surrender—at least for now.

"All right, take a fucking breath and tell me what this is about," he said against my ear. His nearness scrambled and stuttered my senses in the same wonderful collection of seconds. Again, I heeded his command without thinking. "Good," he crooned. "Now breathe again. With me this time."

I felt his powerful chest expand against me as we inhaled and then exhaled together. Once. Twice.

Finally, he turned me to face him. His hands remained on my shoulders. He bent down to align his stare with mine. "Hey there, gorgeous." That damn grin of his, classic Twombley, slid into its cocky, sexy place across his lips. "What's up?"

"I—I left him alone." As soon as I stuttered it, tears clawed up my throat. I gulped to fight them back down, but it was no use. A hot, fat escapee rolled down my cheek. Then another and another. Grant carefully, sweetly, wiped each one away with his thumb. "I'm the worst," I rasped. "I can't even care for a stray cat properly. Robert. He—he needs me, Grant. But I left him!"

Immediately, Grant stood up tall again. He held out his hand for me to take. "Come inside with me for a second."

"But...but..." I thumbed over my shoulder toward the food on the table. "We have breakfast." I sniffled again and wiped my nose with the back of my wrist. "I'd feel terrible to waste all that food, Grant."

"This will just take a second, and then we will eat. Promise. Come on." He gestured with his outstretched hand again, so I took it. Quickly, he was towing me behind him through another part of the boat we hadn't explored on the way out to our first meal.

"I think this will help you, baby." Grant opened a door to a smaller bedroom and stood aside for me to go in, and he quickly closed the door behind us. I gasped the moment I saw the little porcelain dishes on the floor—one with clean water and one with kitten food.

But then my black-and-white friend was brave enough to pop his head out to see who came to visit, and I gasped a second time.

"Grant?" I swung my head around to meet his persistent grin and smoky blue gaze. "You brought him too? Robert?" My knees hit the floor with a *thud,* and I started calling for him. "Kitty kitty kitty?"

Sure enough, when the adorable feline heard my voice, he padded out from his hiding spot under the bed. His little wiry tail went straight to attention as he wove in and out of Grant's long legs, purring as loudly as his young motor could sound.

I laughed in pure delight. Even the cat knew who the most magical person on this boat was.

Impulsively, I bolted upright. Joyously, I threw myself into Grant's arms. Though I hit into him with a *whump,* he easily absorbed the impact and immediately wrapped his strong arms around me. Just as easily, he took the opportunity to nuzzle his face into my neck. He lifted me off my feet and set me up on the bed, where I knelt tall so our stares were much closer to level. I cradled his face in my hands and gazed deeply into his eyes.

Those kind, generous, endless blue eyes . . .

"You're an amazing man, Grant Twombley."

"So I've been told."

I let him have the cocky preen. He certainly deserved it this time. "This was one of the most thoughtful things anyone has ever done for me. Do you know that? I would've never forgiven myself for abandoning him." I just shook my head in pure, stunned bewilderment at this man's thoughtful awareness. "But you knew that. You knew that about me."

"I did," he answered quietly. "I want this trip to be restful and stress-free for you, Rio. I tried to think of everything, but I'm sure I missed something." He gave a panicked look around the cabin as if he were reviewing a mental checklist. "So just remember how happy you are right now when one of those things comes up, 'kay?" He followed his admission with a boyish smile that made my chest ache in an unwelcomed way.

Robert nudged his way between us on the bed, demanding his share of attention and giving me the perfect reason to pull away from the embrace I had so spontaneously entangled myself in. I needed to do my very best to stay out of confusing physical predicaments with this man.

At all costs.

And I could already tell, it wasn't going to be an easy feat. Because I had crystal clear memories of what it felt like to be in his arms. And in his bed. My body recalled exactly how incredible it felt to be mastered by this man's mouth and hands, and good Lord, his—

"Rio?"

"Yeah? Hmm? What?" I looked at him sheepishly. If he could read the thoughts I was just having, he spared my dignity and didn't call me on them.

"Let's go eat," he said. "We can start letting him out of here a little at a time so he can get used to the boat. The crew has a kitty life jacket for him. Once he gets used to wearing it, he can roam about wherever he wants."

I burst out laughing. "Did you just say a kitty life jacket?" Talk about words I'd never thought I'd hear spoken.

"Yes, I did." He even let out a snicker because, seriously, the image conjured was impossible not to laugh at. "But seriously, Rio, have you ever seen a cat try to swim? Not a happy ending, babe." Grant made a scrunched-up face, and even that was adorable, and the inflection in his voice while saying it? I felt like a starry-eyed teenager.

I held my hand up to stop him from going into further detail about swimming cats, though. "No, I know that part," I said while scooting off the bed. I gave Robert one more rub behind the ears before we walked out, promising I'd be back in a bit. "But I'm blown away that you looked into all of this. How did you have time? How long were you really planning all this?"

In a lot of ways, I wasn't sure I wanted to know the answer to that. Had Grant been looking into this charter for a long time? If so, why? Had my eventual meltdown been that obvious—or was his motive threaded into something else? Something like ... desire?

For me?

That last notion got dismissed as soon as we sat down to eat. The simplest answer was usually the truth about something—and for this, the simplest solution also brought the deepest dagger to my chest.

Grant had this floating resort on standby because he'd used it with other women.

Whisked them all away for decadent cruises because he could. And because they were willing and wanton and beautiful. Not frazzled and fucked up and confused.

"Well, Elijah was a lot of help on arranging things," Grant explained while pouring me a glass of juice. "The man has connections you can't imagine. But when I finally nailed down the charter, they asked if there would be pets coming along. That reminded me to go back to your place to get the little guy."

And maybe, just maybe, all of this was really a last-minute thing. I let myself believe it for a little while longer, grinning before I asked, "So . . . you did?" I tacked on a laugh, because the mental image of the Tree in his suit, crawling through my bushes to find Robert, was too delicious to resist.

Grant squashed the vision with a fast head shake. "In the end, Elijah ended up having to do that too—so I could stay with you. Which, of course, I now owe him for, and in a big way."

"Oh no." I giggled harder. "What happened?"

"I don't think they will be exchanging Christmas cards anytime soon, let's just put it that way." He loaded a piece of quiche on his plate and looked to me in question. I shrugged, and he dished me a piece before continuing. "Apparently, Elijah's allergic to cats."

My mouth dropped open. A new gasp tumbled out. "And he didn't tell you?"

"He didn't know," Grant protested.

"Well, crap," I muttered. "I guess he does now?" I slanted a questioning glance his way. "And do I want to know why you're getting so much entertainment out of that?"

"Just the mental image he painted when we talked. Banks is a tough guy, as you've probably figured out by now. The fact that a little fluffy kitty had him sneezing and wheezing and breaking out in hives on his model-perfect skin? I don't know . . . It cracks me up."

I just shook my head, grinning as he laughed harder, telling me the details.

"Makes me sound like an asshole, huh?" He looked abashed, trying to school his features.

"Not really. I've seen the way you guys go at each other."

"Are you going to eat any of that or just push it from one side of your plate to the other?" Grant asked, abruptly changing the subject and bringing the attention to the food I'd been toying with. My stomach just wasn't interested in the fluffy egg pie in front of me.

"Oh, here we go," I said, putting my fork down with a clatter.

"Blaze." He sighed, setting his own fork down with careful grace compared to my toddler tantrum style. "I've said a few times now, this trip is about you relaxing and getting away from the stressors back in LA. But there are a few things I'm going to have to insist on." He held his hand up to tick off the items—finger by long, capable, sexy, and strong finger.

I shook my head a bit to refocus my concentration. Pretty sure his fingers' talents weren't going to be on the list he was about to lay out for me.

"You with me, Blaze?" He chuckled and waited for me to respond. All he got was my best glower, however. He knew damn well what he was doing to me. Scrambling my brain and my libido until I didn't know which one to listen to anymore.

"Can you swim?" I asked breezily.

"You want to go swimming? Now?" He sounded genuinely confused. Not a tone I was treated to very often with this guy.

"No. That's not what I asked."

He thought for a second before answering, "Yeah, I can swim. Why?" He tilted his head a bit, trying to figure out where I was headed with my question.

"Because I'm going to push your ass overboard when you

least expect it. And by the time anyone notices you're gone? You'll have to swim farther than humanly possible, and it will be the perfect crime." I dusted my palms together over my plate as if getting rid of crumbs and then showed him how clean they were. *Innocent until proven guilty*, I mouthed to him, exactly like he had to me earlier.

But instead of being alarmed by my threat, he threw his head back and laughed. That hearty, carefree, spirited laugh with his face tilted up toward the sun in worship.

The kind of careless spirit I envied every time I saw it in another person. And Grant Twombley possessed it in spades. Maybe it's why I was so attracted to him? I hoped just a little of it would rub off on me. A little of that attitude would rain down on me when he seemed to have more than enough to go around. It was infectious.

Wait. No. I was not attracted to this man.

Those traitorous thoughts needed to stay far, far away from my brain and my body at the moment.

As he tempered his laughter to some mild snickering, I expelled a long sigh. Then gave in to an easy smile.

"All right," I finally said. "Fine. Let's hear your fancy boat rules." Like an eager student, I primly folded my hands in front of my plate. But hey, look, no more bites of egg I didn't want in the first place.

He rolled his eyes but copied my pose. "All right, then. Rule one: you have to eat. I'm talking actual food, at least three times a day."

I stared at his index finger standing tall against the azure horizon. Christ, how many torturous rules would I have to endure? If I just nodded along, I'd get this over with quicker and could keep my mind in a safe zone.

I picked up my fork and briskly shoveled another bite of egg into my mouth. I bugged out my eyes and gave him a cheeky smile while I chewed, mumbling "mmmmm!" around the enormous bite I'd just stuffed inside.

Grant shot up a second finger. "You will sleep. I don't care when. But you will sleep at least eight hours total in a twenty-four-hour period. And yes, I'm going to keep track. You need to get back into a healthy sleeping pattern, and if we can do that on this trip without other distractions, you'll thank me for it when we get back home."

I swallowed my food just in time to protest. "Grant, you know how hard that is for me. You can't just tell someone to sleep and it magically happens. You've slept with me before."

Christ. Wrong choice of words.

"You know what I mean," I offered while waving my hand frantically.

"Oh, I know what you mean, baby. And I look forward to that too. But right now, I'm talking about sleeping for restoration. You need that more than anything else. Stop trying to change the subject."

My mouth fell open at his brazen remark, but I couldn't organize a response before he was on to a third demand. Now, his ring finger joined the first two. It had a crooked bend to it at the second knuckle that I hadn't noticed before, almost like it had been broken and never healed right.

He turned his body more toward me before speaking. "This last one you're not going to like. But Rio, it has to be addressed." Grant took a deep breath, and I knew he was nervous about what he was about to say. "Because I don't ever want to relive one single part of yesterday as long as I live. I don't want you to either. You scared the living shit out of me,

Rio Gibson. Do you hear me? I will never unsee the look on your face when I busted into that damn hospital room."

He swallowed so roughly, his Adam's apple bobbed in his throat. The distraction was only momentary, because my protest was already forming on my lips.

"Grant—"

"No!" he said firmly. "I won't accept bullshit on this, girl. I'm serious. I know you have demons. I get that. I accept that. Hell, I fucking understand that. But you have to let me help you. You have to talk to me about what's going on inside here." He carefully leaned forward and tapped on my temple. "You have to at least start by talking to me."

"Fine," I finally conceded. "It's just us out here, after all."

"That's right. And when we get back to Los Angeles, you have to talk to someone who knows how to help you for real." He paused again and then finished with, "A mental health professional."

I shot up from the table with a protest forming on my tongue.

He must have predicted a reaction of the sort though, because he barely flinched. In fact, he calmly had another long drink of his juice as though we were discussing stock dividends from the *Wall Street Journal* while enjoying scones and jam.

"Grant!" I shouted. "Damn it!" If I was going to grandstand, I wanted a fucking audience while I did it.

"Hmmm?" He glanced to me sideways, glass still held aloft.

Sideways! Didn't even turn and look at me straight on, as if he could barely care that I was flipping out just two feet from where he sat.

In a hasty decision, I darted my reach across the table to

try to knock the damn orange juice out of his hand and get the attention I deserved. But he was quicker and saw my move coming. One quick snap of his wrist, and he caught my hand in his and held me with a firm grasp.

Well, at least that got him to set the glass down.

Shit. And prowl toward me. Still gripping my wrist.

A growling sound started down low in his throat before coming out in the form of his question. "What were you thinking just then?"

He towered over me by over a foot, and as I scampered back, he kept advancing, never once surrendering his hold on me. Finally, my back was pressed up against the sliding glass door that led back inside the boat, and I was trapped. I groaned but wasn't sure why. The glass was cool from the air-conditioned space on the other side, compared to the balmy outside air licking across my skin. He moved in until his body was completely flush with mine and raised our clasped hands up over my head until my wrist met the cool glass too. I couldn't take my eyes off the middle of his chest. His breaths were labored and determined, sawing in and out with mesmeric force.

Shiiit—shit! This was so good but so bad. I was so fucked right now.

Was he angry? Or excited, possibly? Because if I wasn't mistaken, there was definitely the start of an erection pressing against me a bit farther south as well.

Grant leaned down until his lips brushed along the curve of my ear. He dragged his tempting mouth back and forth, agonizingly slow a few times before he finally rasped, "Are you testing me on purpose?"

"Graaant," I moaned.

"Is that a yes, Blaze? Push and push and push until I finally snap and do something about this disrespectful mouth and bad attitude of yours?"

Dark lust paralyzed me while he slowly tugged my bottom lip down with the pad of his thumb and then let it snap back into place. I took in an audible breath at the same moment, realizing I'd been denying myself the much-needed oxygen.

"Waiting, baby." He spread his fingers across my cheek. "Is that really what this has come to? Must I really discipline your filthy little mouth?"

Yes. Oh please . . . yes!

I almost said it. Yes, out loud. I yearned to. The acquiescence was a throb in my blood and a bubble in my throat. My vision was consumed by him. My breaths were filled with him. I was drowning in him, and it felt so good . . .

Until it didn't.

Until a bizarre collection of instincts took over. Instincts? Or memories? I couldn't tell. I was blocked from the sunshine. Locked away from the world. Trapped.

Trapped. Trapped!

"No." I squirmed in his grip and got nowhere. "It's a no! We can't do this!"

Panic began to rise up at the feeling of being trapped, and those negative feelings battled with the pleasurable ones that had been driving the horny hormonal bus just a moment before.

He moved his face back, but only by an inch or two. Yep, the situation undoubtedly involved an erection. A firm, insistent cock that was causing me to want things I knew I shouldn't want right now. I shook my head frantically as more confusion heaped onto the pile already swirling inside there.

"Let go!" I said sternly, pushing him. All traces of sexual excitement evaporating like a magic trick.

Grant stepped all the way back. "Okay, baby. Easy." He held up his hands, giving me a wide margin of space. "I'm so sorry, Rio. Honestly."

I bobbed out a nod. "It's . . . fine."

"I didn't mean to . . . I shouldn't have pushed you like that."

"It wasn't all you."

I meant it, though I didn't sound like it. He proved as much by letting his head fall forward and then slowly shaking it. "I'm such an asshole."

"I'd like to take a shower. Will you please show me how to get back to the room I woke up in?" There. That wasn't so hard. I'd be sure to lock every available door in the room and adjoining rooms, and Grant Twombley could handle himself if he still needed a release.

"Yeah, sure. Come on."

As he led me back inside, I concentrated on the layout of the boat. I didn't want to rely on his escort service every time I wanted to do something. It was endearing now, but eventually—and likely rapidly—it would become smothering. Or something similar. Something I was clearly having a problem with processing right now. As amazed and floored as I was by the man's gesture, I wanted—needed—some space to breathe.

"I think everything you need should be in there," Grant said, motioning to the gleaming bathroom off the main stateroom. "I tried to make sure to remember all the brands you use, but—shit, I don't know—you change them all the time." He gave me a sheepish smile, and I felt a pain in my chest I wanted to carve out with a dull knife. What was I doing to this man?

But he went on, clueless to my shameful moment of self-loathing. "If not, we can try to get whatever's missing. Just let me know. Towels are in the cabinet under the sink. And like I said before, there's some clothing that should fit you in the closet there"—he pointed to the built-in storage space along the one side of the room—"and bras, panties, socks, things like that, should be in these drawers." Another wave of his long arm toward the bureau, and the tour was done.

"Oh—okay." It was all I could manage to stammer through. I was equally touched and embarrassed that he had gone through so much trouble. Thinking of the burden I'd been was like trying on a hair suit, and I was having a serious internal struggle with the whole concept. One that just kicked up about twelve notches after the incident outside. If I had one more freak-out, the man in front of me—the one staring at me like he was afraid I was three seconds from exploding like a pipe bomb—would probably elect to dive overboard and swim back to Los Angeles than stay on this luxury yacht with crazy me.

And I couldn't say I'd blame him.

CHAPTER THREE

GRANT

Jesus Christ.

I was the biggest idiot on the planet.

If not that, then the best representative for one of the world's most favorite stereotypes.

I'd really let my dick lead the way this time. Right to my own ruin. At least to my own humiliation—and Rio's disgust. She hadn't pulled any punches about that part.

"And first place for stupid move of the day goes to ..." I paused in my self-directed muttering to beat a soft drum roll on the arm of the main salon's couch. "Yep. Right here, ladies and gentlemen. Step right up and take a swing at the idiot."

I could say it because I meant it. And because nobody from that imaginary mob could beat the brutality of my self-pummeling.

Jesus Christ.

I couldn't even come up with a legitimate reason why I'd gone that direction with Rio. There she was, next to me ... damn near beneath me ... and every switch in my system had flipped. All I could imagine, all I could crave, was making her mine in every carnal way. Dominating her. The instinct took over, as natural as blinking my eyes or scratching an itch.

Scratching a fucking itch?

Another cliché, but worse. Because it was a load of bullshit. Every. Damn. Syllable.

After everything Rio had been through in the past few months—goddammit, the last few days—there was no excuse for pushing her to the point of a panic attack. None.

I'd probably spend the rest of the trip beating myself up for it. And beating off, because there was no way in hell she'd let me near after breaking her trust in that monumental way. She shouldn't.

Oddly, my cell phone ringing broke me out of my self-loathing. Because I assumed we were far from cell service in the middle of the Pacific Ocean, the sound surprised me.

What wasn't surprising? The number of the caller on the small display. Well, this punishment couldn't get any worse than what I was currently putting myself through.

"Hey, Bas. How's it going, man?" I answered as nonchalantly as possible. Never mind that I just skipped town two days ago after breaking his sister-in-law out of the mental health facility his soon-to-be wife had her committed to.

Yep. Just another day in the Shark universe.

"Not like you to ditch work, Grant," my best friend said with an eerie calmness to his voice.

"Didn't you get the voice mail I left you?" I asked, nodding at my casual tone.

"Oh yeah, I got it." There was a heavy pause before he spoke again. "See, here's the thing, though, my friend. We are still friends, Grant, aren't we?"

"Of course we are. Why would you even ask me a question like that?"

Crap. My tone wasn't so casual anymore. Because the thing was... I already knew the answer to my own question.

And was pretty damn sure Bas did too.

"Well, I'm having a hard time separating the truth from the deception at the moment. Seemingly at every turn."

Damn it. Despite the steady underline of his tone, there was no mistaking the bolder strokes of his remark. The determination—and the accusation. With the same collection of words, he was both pissing me off and making me edgy.

Maybe it was time for me to peel my own gloves off.

I elevated my volume a couple of notches while demanding, "What the hell are you talking about?"

"Stop," Bas bit back. "Just stop and cut the shit, Twombley. The damage is already done. Although usually when I find out that a person has lied to me, that's it, you know? I cut him off at the knees. Done."

I drew sharp, incensed air through my nose. "I'm familiar with your standard flow, man." Along with just about every figurative body he'd ever buried on his rise to corporate success. But clearly, His Majesty Shark didn't care to remember that right now.

"Good," he spat. "Because you'll also remember that I don't have room for backstabbers in my life. But when that cut has come from my best friend? No—worse than that—my brother? Well, I don't even know what to do with this information. Not yet, anyway."

"Okay, seriously, man. I'm going to ask you one last time; what the fuck are you talking about?" I huffed in response to his derogatory grunt. "Honestly? You sound like a paranoid prick right now. I haven't lied to you—"

"Ah-ah," he tutted as if chastising a child.

My anger rose another notch as a result of his condescending admonishment. But he didn't even notice the spike in my breathing over the phone. He couldn't see me clenching my free hand into a fist, ready to deck him in his smug face. No, he just continued with his sage advice.

"You may want to think about that claim before making it so emphatically. I warned everyone I'd get to the bottom of what really happened at the Edge job site the night Sean Gibson died. No one fucks me over and gets away with it." His voice grew quiet and full of pain. "I just never thought it would be you, man."

All the shitty events of that night came rushing back to me—in horrifying detail. Racing to the scene to find Rio about to torch the place. Watching her have some sort of psychotic breakdown. Then tackling her to the ground just before she did catastrophic damage to Sebastian's burgeoning building. Finally, trying to clean up the mess she made and enlisting Elijah's help to do so . . .

Shit. Elijah.

I needed to call and warn him before Bas figured out he had any part in this ruse, too. Because like the hunter he was, once Sebastian Shark picked up the scent of blood in the water, he wouldn't stop circling until all the bodies involved were devoured.

"Bas, listen. I can explain. There's so much about that night—"

Click.

A few seconds passed before I was blasted with a dial tone from the other end of the call. The asshole had actually hung up on me!

I sat for long minutes after that, motionless and speechless. Completely lost and beyond confused about what to do with the situation.

My cell seemed to triple in weight as I felt the impact of my best friend's accusation. I didn't want to call him back and grovel for his forgiveness, because frankly, I wasn't sorry. If the exact same thing happened in the next five minutes, I'd likely handle it the same way.

My feelings hadn't changed for Rio since that night. Well, I might have become more ensnared by her complicated, challenging mind. And I might have become more captivated and enchanted by her beauty. I couldn't even allow myself to think about her enticing and alluring sex appeal, or I'd end up in the bathroom with my dick in my fist.

When my cell phone rang again, interrupting my colliding thoughts, I nearly dropped the device in surprise. This time I answered without looking at the caller identification, thankful Bas pulled his head out of his ass and realized he was acting like a child when hanging up on me. I really didn't need more complications in my life right now.

"Dude, I can't believe you hung up on me. Shit." I chuckled. "Seriously, when's the last time you pulled that shit? When we were ten?"

"Grant?" A female's questioning voice filled my ear instead. "Hey, it's Abbigail."

Okay . . . so not who I was expecting, and I was instantly beating myself up for not looking at the device before answering. I definitely did not want to talk to this woman right now.

"How can I help you, Abbi?" I winced at the abrupt shift of my voice, but no way could I muster affection for the person responsible for what I saw Rio having to endure just one day before. Granted, it wasn't the facility specifically. It was imprisoning her in the first place. That was the last thing she needed. Anyone who knew her would know that. I still couldn't understand how Abbigail thought it was the right thing to do.

Regardless of my attitude, her inquisition started straight away. "I'm assuming you know where Rio is? Or you're with her currently?" She only paused long enough to inhale and then continued with her questions. "The facility that I checked her into for psychiatric evaluation and care said she was carried out by a very tall, blond, model-looking man. I'm guessing that was you?"

"Like I asked, Abbi, how can I help you?" My game plan was to give her the least amount of information possible. Rio was a capable adult and was not violating the law or a doctor's orders by leaving that facility.

Abbi sighed loud enough for me to hear this time. "I'm worried about her, Grant," she said softly.

"Okay. Thanks for calling."

"Grant! Wait. Don't hang up."

Her rushed plea torpedoed my intention of ending the call. Damn it. These women were making me soft.

"Please just tell me where you are. Can you just tell me so I can stop worrying? What are your plans?"

I gritted my jaw. "I don't see how that's any of your business."

"But you realize she really needs help, right? She was completely manic the other day at the Abstract kitchen. I've never seen her act that way. Honestly, it really scared me. That's the only reason I reached out for help. I didn't know what else to do."

"Mmm-hmm."

"Grant! You have to believe me!" The predictable tear spigot turned on, and Abbi's watery sniffles accompanied her pleas as the subject had progressively shifted focus to her. Rio had complained about both traits of Abbi's before, and now I was getting a front-row seat to the Abbigail show.

Boy, she and Sebastian were made for one another.

"Actually, Abbigail, I don't have to do anything."

"Grant—"

"You're about to give birth." I was diplomatic but determined, which was going to prevail over her stubbornness and tears. "Maybe it's best that you concentrate on all of that right now and just trust that Rio is in good hands."

A long pause. I even wondered if we'd gotten disconnected, but I didn't try to confirm or hail her.

"Grant, don't be angry," she finally said with the smallest voice.

"Abs, I'm not angry." I laughed and knew I sounded as incensed as I felt. "I'm baffled. How you thought caging her in somewhere was in her best interest—I mean, you say you love her and want what's best for her, yet you do something that is so at odds with her psychological and emotional well-being. Your actions make your words sound more like hollow lip service than anything else."

Again with the long pause, but I knew the connection was fine. And hell, if it wasn't? This conversation was over a while back, as far as I was concerned.

"Well..." she stuttered for a reply. "Well." She sighed heavily, having a tough time with the next part. "Then I made a mistake. Will you just let me talk to her? Please, Grant, is she there?" she asked, and I could hear the waterworks gaining momentum in her shaky voice.

"No, I don't think that's a good idea," I replied resolutely.

"Grant! She's my sister. You can't decide who she talks to and who she doesn't."

Matter-of-factly I replied, "It appears I can." I let that statement hang heavy in the air before going for the finishing move that would secure my spot at the wobbly-legged card table with all the other naughty kids for every holiday meal at Casa Shark, from now until eternity.

Ha! As if I'd ever be invited back to that house!

"Also, Abbigail, she was your sister-in-law, not your sister. But I suppose, technically, she isn't even that anymore, is she? I think it's best you worry about your own life for a while. I don't think you've got what it takes to be making decisions in Rio's. Good luck with everything, though."

After disconnecting the call, I said to the blank phone screen, "You're going to need it," and made my way back to the stateroom. I flopped down and tossed my phone onto the bed. If I were back up on deck, I'd throw the thing overboard after the past two conversations I'd had on the damn device.

"Hey, Tree. What's up?" Rio asked from behind me, startling me out of my fantasy.

I turned to find her standing in the doorway, drying her short hair with a towel. She'd found the fluffy terry robe on the back of the bathroom door and was swaddled in the fresh, white cotton.

With a dismissive gesture toward my phone, I stammered while trying to decide how much to share regarding the call. "Nothing you have to worry about. I bet that shower felt good. How was the water pressure?"

But I should've known better. There was no way she would just let the subject rest if she thought it deserved more attention. Rio would give Bas a warrior's level of competition if tenacity was their chosen battle weapon.

When we spent those first few days in the Abstract prep

kitchen and got under each other's feet as much as we got on one another's nerves, I would tease her and liken her to a stubborn old mule. Remembering those days made my blood heat to the point I tugged on my T-shirt a few times.

"Really, Grant?" She followed the accusation with the curious puppy head tilt I normally loved so much. Except this time the gesture wasn't so cute. "You're asking me about water pressure when you're so tense you look like you could crack walnuts in your fists. You have them balled up like you're ready to punch something."

More like someone.

With determination in her chocolate eyes, she held my focus while closing the distance between us. About a foot of space separated us when I could smell the familiar scent of her shampoo from her damp hair. I greedily inhaled breath after breath through my nose to take in that smell, as if I could store it in my mind for times when she wasn't nearby.

"Your eyes are so blue right now," she commented and leaned back to take in my entire expression. "They get like that when you're dealing with a lot of emotion." She said the words as a statement of fact rather than a question. She knew me better than most other people in my life. But that was just another thing I'd discovered about this woman. She took the time to notice details. Not just about other people but about the world around her. I admired the trait immensely.

Surprising us both, she put her hand on my chest, right over my heart. "What's going on inside here?"

Christ. If you only knew.

But my annoyance with Sebastian and his ladylove had nothing to do with the matters in my heart—so I attempted a careless shrug. Rio let her hand drop away, and I instantly missed the contact. I wanted to feel that same hand slide down my abdomen and then tend to the burning need in my dick. And more ... so much more than that. I was starving for her. My desire pulsed like a strobe light, bright and painful one moment, disarmingly shadowed the next.

But instead, with a heavy sigh, I offered my best explanation. "Some people go through life completely clueless that the world doesn't revolve around them. They can't see past their own shit long enough to realize not everything has to be what's in their best interest. It's frustrating."

"Thank you, Grant," she said quietly, and it was my turn to employ the confused head tilt. Rio pointed to the phone on the bed. "I heard some of that conversation. Not much, but enough to surmise who you were talking to and what it was about. More accurately, who it was about."

"I understand that Abbigail is worried about you. I believe she truly is. But I'm not convinced her intentions are completely altruistic. She's morphing into him with the control bullshit." We both knew who I meant without using his name.

Rio put her hand up to interrupt me. "No, Grant, she's always had control issues. She suffered a terrible loss when her mother died. After that, it was a natural instinct to try to control things to avoid that kind of pain again."

It was hard to understand the depth of this woman's compassion and generosity sometimes. I listened, shaking my head while she basically gave Abbigail a legitimate pass for having her hauled away to that facility. Where did she find this kind of grace?

"What?" She immediately took a defensive attitude. Even her body language reflected it. She popped out one hip and crossed her arms over her chest, adding a sweeping finger up and down the length of my body. "What is this look? Why are you shaking your head?"

"You're an incredible woman, you know that?" Well, that pulled her up short, but she quickly recovered.

In predictable Rio Gibson style, she responded with a sassy comeback.

"Incredibly crazy, apparently. Incredibly unstable and burdensome for the people who get too clo—"

"No," I interrupted. "Stop saying those things. Hear my words, Rio. I was giving you a compliment. Why is that so hard for you to receive?"

"Because that's not how I feel. I don't feel incredible at anything, especially right now. I'm not dumb—or blind. I've noticed the tension between you and your best friend." She looked away, straightening the bedspread to busy her idle hands. "And I hate being the cause of it."

"You're not the cause of it," I protested. "Okay, some of it," I said with a fleeting grin. "But this isn't a new thing. Bas and I don't always see eye to eye. I'm one of the few people in his life who calls him out on his shit."

Rio made a funny face. I detected commiseration laced with conjecture. "My God," she muttered at last. "Can you imagine what an egomaniac that man would be if there was no one to keep him in check?" As if a migraine were brewing behind her brows, she massaged the tension in her forehead. "Let me rephrase that. What kind of an egomaniac—bigger than the one he is now?"

After we both laughed, I said, "Listen, I have an idea."

Rio arched her brow to signal she was waiting, so I went on. "Let's agree to not worry about the Sharks while we are on this boat. Deal? We'll have enough of their drama to deal with when we get back. I'm sure of it."

Rio accepted the hand I proffered, her bow mouth also lifting. "That's a deal," she said, before adding, "And hopefully Abbigail will deliver that child soon, and she'll be obsessing over a new infant instead of me."

Possibly she was reassuring herself more than me at that point, but I couldn't blame her. Abbigail had definitely been in hovering mama hen mode with her lately.

After a longer, semi-awkward moment, she ducked her hands into the robe's pockets and scuffled a little from foot to foot. "In all seriousness though . . . I want to thank you for defending me." She dropped her gaze but not for long. As if reminding herself of the importance of what she had to say, she jolted her gaze back up to mine. "And not just right now, on the phone with both halves of the dynamic duo."

I knitted my brows together. "I'm not following." And I meant it.

"Come on, Grant. There have been other times than this. Times that I don't know about. I know what people must be saying about me behind my back—and I'm guessing you've come to my defense then, too."

"Blaze," I muttered, rubbing the back of my neck.

"Don't 'Blaze' me. Just accept my gratitude."

I didn't comply. Instead, I reached forward and tugged her closer. Closer. I couldn't help myself. I needed to touch her. Despite all the promises I'd just made myself, I needed the physical connection. The contact with her and only her. Especially as she stood in front of me, looking as unsure as a little girl on her first day of school.

I simply had to wrap my arms all the way around her.

Thankfully, she let me.

I pulled her flush against my body and rested my cheek on top of her head. It felt as good to shield her physically as it did verbally. What could I do to get her used to the idea too? The idea of us, as more than just occasional phone calls and walls that came down only when we were desperate or drunk.

Things could be so good between us.

So damn good.

I could take care of her in more ways—in all the ways. But right now, that was just a fantasy in my mind, set on hopeless repeat.

But I had hope. Lots of it. Especially this moment.

Assuredly after I dropped the next—and more concerning—issue from Sebastian's phone call, she'd realize just how loyal I was. How thoroughly I could be her ultimate safety zone.

"Blaze?"

"Hmmm?"

"I have to talk to you about one more thing. Something that came up during my conversation with Sebastian. As much as I don't want to get you wound up with it, I can't in good conscience keep anything from you either."

Rio sat down on the edge of the bed, instantly looking exhausted. "Geez, Grant, with a lead-in like that, I can't wait to hear what you're about to say." She chuckled sarcastically.

"I know, baby, I'm sorry. I really considered not talking with you about this, but that just doesn't feel right. You can handle it though. It's actually not new news. Not technically." Maybe if I acted like I wasn't that concerned, my calmness would flow through to her too. A guy could dream, right?

With a wave of her hand, she motioned to get on with it. "Let's hear it."

"Sebastian was the first one who called just now. And he insists he's gotten to the bottom of the fire residue that was left behind at Sean's accident scene."

"The man is like a dog with a bone. I'd think he would have more important things to do with his day," she said.

"Right?" I agreed with her thought. "Well, anyway, he's indirectly implying you had something to do with it, and he has himself convinced I covered your tracks. I tried to get more details from him, and the bastard hung up on me." I shook my head in disbelief. Recounting the story made it seem that much more ridiculous. "He fucking hung up on me."

I looked up from where I'd been toeing the base of the bed frame while I spoke. The expression on Rio's face was not what I expected. Instead of outrage on my behalf or worry for her own safety and legal standing, I was met with a completely blank stare. A few silent moments passed before I shifted my weight from one foot to the other. Maybe she was letting it all sink in before her reactionary outburst. A few seconds more, and still, she just stared off into space.

"Rio?"

With a little flinch, she finally focused on me again. "Hmm? What?" she asked.

"Aren't you going to say something?" One Mississippi. Two Mississippi. Three—no, fuck this!

"Rio!" I said sternly.

"What?"

"I don't know. I thought you'd say something about what I just told you, but you're staring off into space like you're stoned. I mean, I get that it's probably causing some anxiety or stress or whatever—" I dropped my shoulders, feeling so lost on how to deal with this woman. "Just talk to me."

Restless, she stood and answered, "What's there to talk about? If he knows, then he knows. It's not like he's far from the truth, Grant. Sebastian Shark can prosecute me, and then the police and lawyers can decide what happens from there." Rio shrugged then, like she didn't have a care in the world. "You're really making more of an issue out of this than it needs to be."

With that declaration, she detoured around where I stood and went to riffle through the clothes hanging inside the closet. I'd had my assistant shop for the typical concert tees and jeans she favored, a couple sundresses, a bathing suit, and a few pairs of pajamas. I figured if she needed anything else, we could get it when we hit the port in Hawaii.

Every instinct in my body shouted at me to just let it go. *Don't make such a big deal out of the bomb Bas just dropped on you and carry on with our day.* This was supposed to be a stress-free break for her, after all.

But a strange mix of fury and frustration brewed in my blood. That odd combination, along with my sexual frustration, made my fuse shorter than usual. I wanted to pummel someone—or something.

Because, goddammit, I just might have ruined a lifelong bond with one of the two friends in my orbit I considered family.

And I did it for her—to protect her.

To ensure that she could work through her issues in freedom, not a jail cell.

And yes, I'd do it all again. Every single decision.

At the moment, however, I needed to work out the built-up frustration I was caging and come back to her in a calmer physical state and with a more rational mental one as well.

"I think I'm going to go work out for a little while. Will you be okay on your own for an hour or two?"

"For Christ's sake, Grant. I'm a grown woman. Plus, it's not like I can go anywhere." Her features softened while she tried to reassure me. "I'll be fine. I'll probably catch up on email and stuff. Do you mind if I use your laptop to sign in to my account?"

"No, I don't mind. I'll get it set up for you. There's a small office at the bow of the boat. Do you want to go there? Maybe have a little change of scenery? I can show you how to get to the cat's cabin on the way."

"Actually, I think I'll just stay here. Maybe take a little nap too."

"All right, suit yourself. When I get back, we can decide how to spend the rest of the day," I said, pulling a tank top on while I spoke. There was no way I was going to let her stay cooped up in this cabin for the next week. Rio, me, and a giant bed plus an endless amount of time was not a safe equation to calculate at the moment. No, it was outright perilous.

For the first time since meeting this intriguing, confusing, challenging woman, I feared I might be in over my head.

CHAPTER FOUR

RIO

Only twenty-six messages waited in my email inbox. That was unusual, but I assumed Abbi had asked Dori to handle all the Abstract Catering correspondence, because not a single message was from that address.

I scrolled down the column anyway, curious about what kind of crap had made it through the junk mail filter.

Huge Going Out of Business Sale!

Delete.

"Didn't they already go out of business months ago?" I muttered.

Travel Deals You Can't Pass Up!

Delete.

Sorry, gang. Can't make it to Aruba or Cairo this year. Want to know about my yacht cruise to Hawaii, though?

Mmm . . . with a cruisemate who looked so damn sexy in board shorts, I was four seconds from jumping him.

"Move on, girl," I ordered myself through gritted teeth.

Genius Brain Update: Install Now!

Delete.

I'd removed that silly app an hour after downloading it—yet had been dealing with the promotional emails for eight months since. It was a little creepy—unless the damn app knew something I didn't. Maybe I did need a few more genius neurons in my skull. Maybe they could've helped me from landing in this exact predicament.

"Move. On." Forget the mutter. I fully growled it at myself now.

Top Ten Reasons Not to F$%* Your BFF.

"Well, here we go! Finally something with promise."

My favorite online magazine subscription was one of my guilty pleasures, an ideal distraction for my overactive mind. Between the fluffy articles, horoscope predictions, trending top tens, and pop-up advertisements, there were also many helpful advice columns. After a few clicks of the trackpad, I had this one loaded and ready.

Too bad the end result wasn't as good as my anticipation. The article ended up being snarky, bitter, and disappointing. Maybe the author was fresh off a bad breakup. Or maybe her partner went to work one day and never came home.

Like mine.

So who was the bitter one now?

I wasn't about to answer that. Besides, I'd given enough time to cyberspace already. I quit the browser, logged out of my email account, and closed the lid of Grant's laptop. My eyes were getting heavy while I read that drivel anyway, so a nap seemed like the right call. The cabin was so warm and quiet, making it easy to relax on top of the covers and curl up on my side.

And just like that, sleep was impossible.

Cue the racing thoughts.

Like wisps from a windblown dandelion, one topic after another darted over my brain's hills and valleys, making it difficult to focus on just one—until a major seedling started blowing by more than the others.

Still, I desperately tried to ignore it.

"Shit." I sighed.

I had to think about what had happened at Clear Horizons, as well as before, and after.

Analyzing my behavior the day Abbigail had me carted off to that place had to be done. Yes, *that* place. Christ, I couldn't even think of its name without getting chafed. My mind had been anything but clear that day, or even the few preceding it. All right, so maybe I hadn't been sensible for a long while—but knowing I was considered that unstable and dangerous to the people around me, my very family and loved ones, was past the point of unsettling. Throughout the years—fine, my entire life—I'd struggled with staying in optimum mental health. The social stigma attached to being diagnosed with a mental health disorder hadn't helped either. But I would never hurt another person. No. There'd always been just one target of my abuse.

Me.

If there were an award for self-doubt and self-recrimination, I'd win hands down. Year after year, I would be the top of the heap at hating myself and everything about me. Of course, to the outside world, I didn't appear insecure or fragile. Those particular flaws were hidden by a mask that had been carefully constructed over the years. I had perfected the art of the sham. Fake it until you make it—and look good while doing so.

Next, the unnecessary apology. Also, a professional in that arena. Shamefully, I can admit to apologizing for apologizing. All while maintaining it was perfectly rational to do so. Routinely, people forgave me for things I haven't even done. The trick was to believe the nonsense yourself, so the sell was authentic. I was convinced I was responsible for every adverse action and reaction within a five-mile radius at all times. Just a precious gift my mother bestowed upon me when I was very young. She adopted the awesome parenting style of guilt as guidance, and I always took the bait. After all, at that age, every child wants to please their parent. If that meant feeling bad for every wrong or bad thing that happened, often encouraged by her insults and misplaced anger, then that's what I did! I was committed to the cause and excelled. Who could blame a girl for doing her best?

Identifying my flaws had never been a problem. Figuring out how to quit the bad habits afterward had been the real issue. That, and believing I was worth finding a solution in the first place. Throughout my life, I'd spent more money on therapist office visits than most people do on groceries. Yet there I was, freshly sprung from a mental health care facility like an ordinary convict.

Shit. I even failed at being crazy.

A click in the doorknob warned me Grant was back.

I was lying with my face turned away from the door, so I relaxed my breathing and slid my eyes shut, feigning sleep in hopes he'd peek in and leave. Not an easy feat, considering Grant Twombley seemed to shrink a room just by entering it. His imposing height, confident strength, and charismatic presence eclipsed everyone and everything else. Surely I wasn't the only one who knew that about the man, though I was certainly the human benefiting—suffering?—from it as he came all the way into the cabin, moving closer by quiet steps.

With equal grace, he slid his full body onto the bed behind me.

Damn it!

My eyes popped open, and I was careful not to sharply inhale from the sudden shortage of oxygen in my blood.

There he went again, slicing every air molecule in half. That was only what he did to the atmosphere *outside* my body. Inside, I was roiling heat—and inescapable confusion.

Why was he back in here so fast?

According to the man himself, he had a ton of work piling up, yet I hadn't seen him check his phone outside the calls he took from Sebastian and Abbi. Had he already finished with his professional obligations as well as his workout?

And right now, with him so achingly near, did I really care if he had?

I didn't bother answering myself on that one either. I wanted to savor every millisecond of this moment instead.

Grant didn't move any closer. Nor did he make a move to touch me. He simply shared his comforting warmth by being near. It was part of the reason I couldn't seem to stay away from him. He could calm me when no one else could. It was such a gift he gave to me, part of this unusual, phenomenal pull between us...a connection that I'd never had with another human. A treasure I never wanted to part with.

I often wondered...did he feel it too? He had to, at least in some measure. His forbearance sure as hell didn't escape my notice. No matter how much resistance I threw at him or how many times I pushed him away, he never really budged. When it seemed like everything else in my life had been turned upside down, he was my constant.

Ten minutes went by—I was watching the clock on the nightstand—in which both of us were still and simple in our sublime silence. Finally, I gave into the pull and rolled to my back to look fully at him.

He kept his eyes closed as if he were sleeping too, and I took the rare opportunity to stare at him. His hair was damp, but he smelled fresh, like old-fashioned bar soap. Nothing fancy from a mall specialty store like he normally used, just pure and natural, and it still suited him. His beard was growing in, but not too dark. Since his hair was naturally blond, his whiskers were light too. That morning, while out on the sunny deck, I noticed a bit of auburn in the stubble too.

He had such wholesome good looks, with his formidable cheekbones and defined brow bone, but beneath was a wicked and filthy mind. His mouth—Lord, his mouth—and the rest of his body could deliver on all the dirty promises that clever brain came up with. I pressed my legs together subtly, not wanting to shift too much weight on the mattress. There was a good chance he wasn't really sleeping, but in case he had drifted off, my sexual frustration was not going to be what woke him.

Still, my hand burned to touch him. The longer I stared, the more insistent the need became. I wanted to feel his firm skin beneath my fingers and run them through his thick hair. The sun had kissed the prominent angles of his face, and he had a promising start to a golden tan. I let my gaze roam down his corded neck to his broad chest. Thankfully he'd put a regular T-shirt on after showering, because the tank top he'd had on to work out would've been the death of me. Nevertheless, the tee provided a perfect showcase for his strong arms, ending with long, skillful fingers tipped by perfectly manicured nails.

Just thinking of him wrapping those arms around me again…touching me…stroking me…pleasuring me…Nirvana.

My breath stuttered when his cheek twitched, and I watched as it became a devilish grin. It took every effort to hold in my own guilty giggle, knowing I was busted.

Without opening his eyes, he asked in a low, husky voice, "Like what you see, Blaze?"

"Sleeping," I mumbled as a last-ditch effort to get away with having stared at him for the past ten minutes.

"Bullshit." He chuckled, grin growing wider. "You've been undressing me in your imagination since you rolled over. Don't lie about it."

God help me, somehow he looked even sexier than before.

Grant Twombley wore confidence like a second skin. The guy was tall, fit, and ridiculously attractive, and he knew it. He dressed like a fashion model, had the money of a king and the carefree attitude of a prince. Yet for some unexplainable reason, he was deeply invested in me. While many women would sell their soul for the dream, most of the time, I felt like his charity pet project. His version of giving back to humanity. Heal the broken girl's heart and mind and secure your place just to the right of the highest.

"Well?" he prompted. "Are you going to answer me?"

"You're definitely easy on the eyes, Tree. But you know that already. All your little fangirls feed your ego enough—you don't need me to do it too. Do you?"

Yeah, so it was a tactic. But I'd worked the anger-over-arousal angle with him before and went all-in on it working again now. Though after a few moments, I wondered if he was going to be the issue here. Being this close to him, with our bodies stretched out and nearly touching…the proximity wasn't as easy as it once was. Not by half. His powerful poise, leonine grace, and sensual self-awareness were like catnip to this starving kitty.

He finally opened his eyes, and I fell into the blue pools. My breathing kicked up as I watched him assess me from head to toe. My sexual frustration was a living, breathing thing between us on the plush bed.

"Blaze," he almost moaned, and an audible gasp tumbled from my lips in response.

Without embarrassment, he freed the hand that had been between his head and pillow and reached into the elastic band of his shorts and palmed his erection. It was impossible to miss in the soft, yielding fabric of his athletic shorts, but I had been doing my level best to not let my eyes drift below his collar. Now, he was drawing a giant neon arrow down there.

I gasped again. His groan was doubly gruff as before, especially as he blatantly gripped himself. As I watched, rapt and hypnotized.

"Baby, I'm sorry, but I'm dying here. All I can think about is the heat of your pussy around my cock. Lying this close to you without touching you…" He flared his nostrils when he inhaled and said, "Shit, I will beg if it means feeling you again." With eyes as dark as the midnight ocean, he studied me.

I was frozen where I lay, so unsure about the right thing to do.

Finally, I rasped, "Show me." The two words were all I could manage through the thick lust constricting my throat.

"What?" he asked and then swallowed so roughly I almost burst into flames watching his throat contract with masculine power. "Show you what?" he asked then, maybe wanting to make sure he wasn't falsely hoping I'd said something I didn't.

"I want to watch you come. I want to see you grip yourself and get yourself off."

One side of his luscious mouth inched up. "Are you sure you don't want to help?"

"No," I answered, meeting his hungry look with a matching one of my own. "You."

"What about you? What will you be doing while I beat off for you, Rio?"

I shrugged. The details of my brazen plan weren't that thought out. I just knew I wanted to push him to his limit. But wanting to seem like more of a vixen than that, I said, "I'm not sure. Maybe I'll use my mouth just before you come. I haven't decided yet."

He tugged his shorts and boxers down before helping me shimmy the bed's comforter down to the floor.

"Where do you want me? Beside you? Over you? Tell me." He fisted his shaft aggressively and began stroking. "Wet my hand." He held his palm out to me, leaving the *how* for me to decide. God, I could barely unscramble my thoughts enough to take action.

"Rio," he said in the darker timbre his voice naturally shifted to in the bedroom. "Help me." He thrust his upturned palm closer, so I leaned in and licked his upturned hand from the tip of his middle finger to the fleshy part of his palm. I kept my eyes pinned to his while I hovered over the center and let as much saliva that I could quickly pool together slowly dribble from my mouth to his receiving hand.

"Fucking hell, woman," he groaned and then inspected my deposit. He added more of his own spit to the small amount on his palm and coated it over his cock. The tight skin was slick and shiny from our combined efforts, and he began roughly stroking. The muscles in his forearm bunched and flexed as he moved from the base to the full crown.

The image would be burned in my memory for all time. A visual treasure I would likely use to pleasure myself from here on.

"Holy shit," I whispered, momentarily concerned I would have an orgasm of my own from just watching the erotic show in front of me. Impulsively, I pulled my shirt up and over my head and then reached for the clasp of my bra at the center of my spine. He had purchased some beautiful lingerie for me to wear, and I currently wore a matching set in bloodred lace and satin.

"No," Grant growled. "Leave it on." His greedy gaze swept my body from top to bottom several times before he added, "I love that color against your pale skin. Fuck . . . yes!"

The last of it groaned by my sexy lover as I scratched my fingernails up and down his thigh. To ensure I didn't miss one moment of his pleasure, I lay on my side and propped my head up on a bent elbow. "Jesus, Grant. You are so hot right now."

"Are you wet? Does it turn you on to see how hard I am because of you?"

"Shit, yes, I am. Soaked, actually." I still had my jeans on, so I opened the single button and zipper and spread the material as far as it would part.

"No, all of it," he demanded. "Show me your cunt," he issued with erotic urgency.

"No." With a shake of my head, I purred, "Not until you come. Are you close? Would you rather have my mouth sucking you off while you finish or my pussy clenching around you?" I stroked my tight nipples through the red lace and sighed at the contact. Where the hell was this sex kitten bravery coming from? But did I really want to analyze that answer right now? "Oh God, yes, so good," I continued, just enjoying the genesis of this new, naughty creature inside me. "You're going to come so hard, aren't you?"

"Christ," Grant choked. "I'm going to come. Where? Where do you want it, Blaze? Tell me!"

"Here." I swirled my finger in a circle on my stomach, drawing in slowly toward my navel. "Let me feel it all, Grant. Please. I need to," I panted. "I need to feel you." I arched my back off the bed as if in the throes of an epic orgasm myself. Hopefully, the pose created alluring curves to my otherwise stick-straight body. The crimson panties peeked out from my untethered jeans. Three crisscross strips hugged my hips, making me feel beautiful and sexy at the same time.

Grant's deep, throaty groan was the only warning before he spurted warm, milky semen across my stomach and rib cage. "Jesus. Christ. Fuck. Fuck." The perfect man continued to kneel over me as he lazily stroked himself a few more times. His entire body shuddered with the sensations of completion before he let his head hang with a deep, satisfied inhalation.

I gave in to the intense impulse to run my fingers through his fluid that decorated my skin. With the index finger extended, I slowly moved my hand down my body while taking advantage of the chance to track Grant's hooded stare as he followed my every move.

"Now you," he said then, his blue eyes sparking with unquenched lust.

"You don't have to do anything. That was amazing to watch."

"No, I need to, girl. I need to taste you on my tongue," he said, standing from the bed.

"Where are you going? Just lie with me awhile." But I spoke to empty air then, when he disappeared into the bathroom and then quickly returned with the hand towel that normally hung beside the sink.

"Let's clean this off." He wiped his semen from my stomach and tossed the towel behind him. His gaze never left my body. His erection was already heavy and full, as though he hadn't been remotely satiated by masturbating.

"These need to go," he grunted and pulled my jeans from the hem. "Lift up a second," he instructed, tugging with powerful efficiency and then adding my pants to the other discarded items on the floor. "Fucking hell, baby. These panties." He swept his gaze from the satin-and-lace fabric up to mine. "You good with this? I don't want anything you don't want."

"I'm good," I whispered.

And just like that, my resolve to keep him at arm's length faded away like the last notes of a melancholy song. The words *physical need* beat on my conscience's drum instead. These were just physical needs being satisfied between two people. Nothing more.

Nothing more.

Warm breath brought my focus from my guilt-laden thoughts to the sex god poised between my thighs. Those damn blue eyes watched every thought, every emotion, every desire that broadcast across my face while I waited for him to make contact. I scooted back so my torso was propped up by the generous pillow pile on the bed. Watching him work his tongue magic was as erotic as feeling it.

"Comfy now?" He grinned mischievously and then winked.

For Christ's sake, this guy. The panties we were both in

love with were going to melt right off my body if he kept up the devilish, playful bit. I loved this side of him, and if possible, it added to his allure.

"Yes, thank you." I smiled too. To spur him into action, I added, "I like seeing your mouth on me. When all I see is the top of your head, because you're so into your task, your entire face is buried." When I finished painting that picture, I rolled my eyes and dropped my head back into the pillows.

"You're killing me, baby. These were a great choice, huh?" He brushed his knuckles against my swollen clit through the fabric, and I moaned. "Fuck, Rio, look how ramped up you are. Your clit is so needy that I can see the shape of it through your panties."

His words and his touch were going to send me over the edge. I sucked in air through my nose and let my eyes drift closed.

One more stroke, just one more…

"Oh no, you don't." He chuckled and stilled his hand, and I whimpered in frustration. "I definitely need my lips and tongue and teeth on you when you come." To accomplish that, he gripped the delicate strips at my hips and peeled off the undies.

"Graaanntt." I drew out the single syllable of his name and complained, "Please! Shit, I was so close. That's just cruel."

"Mmmm," was all he said while nestling back between my legs. He finger-painted my sensitive sex with his index finger by dragging my own slickness around in slow, torturous circles. "So sexy, Blaze. You're so wet… so hot. Fuck, I have dreams about this pussy."

"Is that so?" I asked in lighthearted disbelief. Quickly, everything changed, however. From playful to overwhelmingly stimulating in seconds. My brain swam with endorphins, and my skin broke out in chill bumps when he finally took the first pass with his tongue.

Grant worked at my needy button with his flat tongue. Swipe after swipe, repeating the same motion in an intoxicating rhythm. I dug my fingers into his lush hair and moaned.

"So good. It's so good, Grant. Don't stop. Please don't stop. I'm so close, God, yes!"

When he entered me with his expert fingers, I was done. After just watching him beat off, then adding his mind-numbing oral skills, I was primed to orgasm in record time. When the climax broke free, my entire body tensed with the prickling pleasure of every nerve ending firing at once. Every muscle contracted in unison too.

The beautiful man crawled over me and braced his weight on his bent arms positioned on either side of my head. After recovering from the all-consuming rush of my release, I smiled up at him and thanked him.

"Oh baby, you don't have to thank me for eating your pussy. I'd happily make the experience my chosen career path if it actually paid my bills."

His ridiculous comment brought a giggle all the way up from my heart. It felt so good to be so buoyant, even if just for a moment.

Grant's thick erection was pressed between us and twitched and pulsed with need. He rolled his hips into my cleft, and my sensitive sex all but cried to be filled. I'd sworn I wouldn't sleep with this man again until I had my head on straight, yet here I was. Beneath him and all but begging to be stuffed with his cock.

"Oh God, why does that have to feel so good?" I couldn't

look at him directly, but with his proximity, it was difficult to look anywhere else, so I closed my eyes instead. With his face nuzzled into the junction of my neck and shoulder, his groan vibrated through to my core.

"Blaze. I want to be inside you more than my next breath. The heat coming off your pussy right now is killing me. Fuck." He rotated his hips again. "Fuck, baby. Can you feel that? The way you're making my cock so slippery. Fucking perfection." He stilled his movement and pulled back to look at my face. "Are we doing this?"

Who was I trying to kid? Of course he would get what he wanted. Because I wanted it too. Wanted him to the point of feeling pain at the thought of not having him. There would be plenty of time afterward to beat me up for complicating things between us again. Finally, I gave a quick nod, and he covered my mouth with his.

But Grant Twombley didn't kiss. He took. Stole. Robbed me of every rational thought and swept me up in the tide of his lust. I was pulled under with every masterful invasion of his tongue and every demanding nip of his teeth. Along my jaw. Behind my ear. Down my throat. With his mouth, he explored every inch of my body that he could reach. My pussy reacted by weeping more for his erection.

"Fuck me, Grant," I panted breathlessly. "Put your dick in me and fuck me. God! Please!" I begged into the sultry air of the room. Apparently, those were the words he'd been waiting to hear. As soon as I finished pleading, he reached between our bodies and directed the head of his shaft to my opening. He ensured we had firm eye contact before sliding into me completely.

"Fuck, baby. So good. It's so good in this cunt. I'm ruined

for any other." Slowly withdrawing, he kissed me again. Expert strokes followed, and both our control began to slip. I gasped when he moaned. I sighed when he growled. Erotic sounds from our throats and lewd, wet sounds between our bodies echoed around the room. My head spun with the exquisiteness of it all.

"Rio. Baby. Come with me. God, I can't hold it off," Grant panted while pounding into me.

"Don't stop. Don't stop. Yes! So close," I answered through my own ragged breaths.

Together we reached our peak, and he went utterly still, absorbing the way our bodies held each other in the tightest, pulsing, and throbbing embrace.

The wonder in my voice was pure when I looked at him and said, "I feel you. I can feel you coming inside me."

"I know, baby, feels so good." His eyes drifted closed, and he groaned as I clenched my insides around him. "Yes, God. Squeeze me like that. Fuck, that's amazing. I think I'm getting hard again." He kissed my nose and grinned down at me. "You are so incredible. Do you know that?" A slight shift of his hips, and he pulled out of my pussy and rolled to the side, pulling me against him when he settled on the mattress.

And then silence. Golden silence. There were times—notably, when my anxiety was ramped up—that silence was louder than a brass band. But lying in Grant's embrace, while he delivered an occasional kiss to my shoulder, neck, even my hair, peace blanketed the room. A girl could get used to feeling safe in his arms.

Don't go there, fool.

Sex was sex. Just physical need, and nothing more. I was in no place, emotionally or psychologically, to consider what just happened between us as anything more. Nothing but trouble would result from that dangerous line of thinking. Grant was a terminal bachelor. I knew I was already breaking the mold of his usual conquests when he dipped his dick in me more than the one time. The interest he took in me was so outside his normal behavior. Those were the facts I needed to remind myself of—and often.

"Should we shower?" he asked quietly.

"Probably," I replied, but neither of us made a move to get up. His muscular arm was slung across my waist and I rested mine on top. "Let's just chill here for a bit. Feels too comfortable to get up."

"Agreed."

This time when the silence settled, I could feel the weight of his unspoken thoughts. My curious mind weighed the merits of asking him what he was thinking so intensely about. But I knew how cliché it would sound from a freshly fucked female to ask this brooding male, "What are you thinking about?" Nine times out of ten in this situation, hearts and egos were stomped on. The answer might not be one I wanted to hear.

Fuck it. When had I ever played on the safe side of the tracks? So, throwing caution to the wind, I asked him, "What's so heavy on your mind, Twombley? I can feel the weight of your thoughts hanging above us like an anvil." I stroked up and down his arm, trying to let him know I wasn't looking for a confrontation.

Long minutes passed, and he didn't respond, even though I could tell from his restless shifting he hadn't drifted off to sleep. Just when I was giving up on having my question answered, he pulled his arm off my body and rolled over to face me, resting his cheek on his folded hands.

I mirrored his pose, although skipped the prayer-hands pillow. Maybe I shouldn't have though. Divine strength could've helped while I waited for him to organize his thoughts.

"You've been hanging around me too much," I finally teased to ease the burden of the moment.

He eyed me carefully and asked, "What do you mean?"

"You're overthinking something on a professional level. Analytical skills like that take years to develop. You're not typically the one who beats everything to death around here. That's totally my gig, and you're stealing my thunder."

Grant chuckled then but still didn't give up a clue as to what the problem was.

"Don't your hands fall asleep when you lie on them like that?" I asked. "That would drive me crazy, and you always lie that way."

He grimaced and repositioned himself to sit up against the upholstered headboard. "It's a dumb habit I can't shake." He popped all the knuckles on one hand, then the other—another ritual I'd seen him perform countless times after lying down.

"So, it does bother your hands. Because you crack your knuckles then, too."

"You're like a dog with a bone today, Ms. Gibson."

Frustrated, I said, "You know so much about me. Would it kill you to share one little thing? Be a little vulnerable?" There was accusation in my tone, I heard it myself, but I couldn't feel at all remorseful for it. So many of my dirty secrets were like living, breathing things between us.

The man rolled his eyes and let out a sufferable sigh. "It's not that fascinating, Rio, trust me." Another minute went by before he finally decided to continue. "I was the unfortunate reckless result of an incurable drug addict who slept around for drug money. I never met my father." He shrugged as though it didn't matter, but I saw the pain in his normally lively eyes. Saw the way his throat worked to manage his next couple of swallows. "She said it could've been any one of a handful of guys. Nice, huh?"

I sat up and folded my legs beneath me. The impulse to hold him while he told me about his childhood, hug him at the very least, was overwhelming. But interrupting seemed like the quickest way to end this unique peek into his history.

"When things were good, we had a roof over our heads, but that didn't necessarily mean she was paying for it. So it didn't usually last. I slept on more floors, dirty mattresses, and eventually, alleyways, that I just got in the habit of cushioning the discomfort with my hands. Not to mention the filth and God knows what else."

"Oh, Grant," I choked out.

"Don't."

"What, don't?" I mocked his solemn voice while standing from the bed, intending to fetch the cozy robe from the bathroom.

"I don't want or need your . . ."

But when I looked back to Grant to see if he was going to finish what he was saying, the look on his face had me freeze where I stood. All his angst had disappeared. Pure lust replaced it. Lust and another emotion. But I couldn't work out exactly what that was.

"Christ, woman," he growled while sitting up taller.

"What?"

"Look at you." Chest pumped with sexual intention. "Fucking perfection, Rio."

"Come on, be serious" was all I could say. Panicking, I

dashed into the bathroom and gripped the edge of the counter. I took a few fortifying breaths for courage while I donned the robe. Securing the belt around my waist, I reentered the bedroom area of the cabin.

"You scared me there for a second," I said, as if none of that had just happened. "I thought something was really wrong the way your face changed so quickly." I flopped down on the bed by his feet. "But seriously, do you want to talk about all of that?"

He stared at me for another long moment until I began to squirm in discomfort from his laser-focused attention. Finally, the man said, "I was completely serious. My reaction to your naked body was genuine. But now all I can think about is what it would take to get you back under the covers with me so I can fuck you again. And again." Ice-blue eyes bored directly into my core while he spoke.

I fluttered my hand to my chest because my heart felt like it was about to break free. His husky tone and carnal glare made my pussy throb at the same galloping pace.

But I had to keep myself in check. Had to be responsible and level-headed. Except being those things were the exact opposite of how I truly felt. At some point, fighting the natural pull between us would be too much for me. I could already feel my resolve crumbling, and it was only the first day we were trapped on this boat together.

My sanity was just pushed overboard by my libido, who stood on deck clutching the life ring and wearing a lazy grin. I already knew who my pussy would save first, because that lady was an expert swimmer. Hell, when it came to Grant Twombley, the traitor could do all four strokes with the skill of an Olympian.

Yeeaah . . . I was so fucked.

CHAPTER FIVE

GRANT

What was this woman doing to me? Seriously. How did she whittle through my normally impenetrable veneer and see right to my truth? Usually, I could hide my genuine emotions. It was a skill that was meticulously honed as a young boy because my mother was an opportunist. If that woman noticed I was particularly fond of something, that was the first thing she sold. After all, drug money didn't come easily to the terminally unemployed. If she witnessed me having a close friendship with another kid, he was the one I was forbidden to see. "When you let people get too close, they exploit your weaknesses," she preached. The truth was she wanted to be the main focus of my attention and love. Always. Her insecurities ran so deeply, even another child in my orbit threatened her. All that and the low-quality meth she smoked, snorted, or on occasion shot into a vein made her paranoid. It was all shitty behavior for a grown woman playing her hand at Mommy and all so sad when I thought about it as an adult.

So fucking sad.

"You good, Tree?" Rio, who was still perched by my feet on the bed, tweaked my big toe, and I gave my head a little shake.

Begone, ghosts of shitty past!

"Yeah, sorry. For some reason, my head is all over the

place right now," I said softly.

"Maybe because you never just take time to unwind?" Rio proposed. "Think about it. When's the last time you took a vacation? Even a long weekend and just did something other than Sebastian Shark's bidding?"

"I don't do his bidding," I scoffed.

She let her head flop over to one side and gave me a look that screamed, "Bullshit." And yeah, she was probably right, but I wasn't about to admit that to her.

Instead, feeling defensive, I nearly spat, "My job involves a lot more than doing what Bas tells me to do. I have responsibilities completely independent of him." With that, I swung my legs off the bed and searched for my clothes. I wasn't typically uncomfortable being naked around her, but something about that comment had me feeling vulnerable and insecure. Two more feelings I wasn't familiar with. Again, I asked myself, how was she doing this? What was it about Rio Gibson that brought out emotions I buried long, long ago? Feelings I had no interest in suffering through now, either.

My shorts and boxers were in a twisted heap beside the bed, and I had to take a moment to untangle the garments before I could put them back on. Frustrated, I jammed my legs in and yanked them into place, glaring at the floor while doing so.

"Hey..." she said quietly, and when I didn't meet her gaze, she spoke my name in that lush, husky tone that made my pulse spike. "Grant." She waited until I found her whiskey stare. "What's going on? What did I say that pissed you off?"

"I'm not pissed," I said, wincing at the petulance in my tone.

"Come on." She paused, and I thought she'd drop it there.

But no such luck. The woman continued pressing me instead. "Normally, you're much more agreeable after sex. Something's definitely got your pants in a bunch. Literally." Her soft smile turned to a giggle as we both looked down to see I had yanked my shorts on backward.

With a heavy sigh, I sank back onto the bed beside her to fix my clothes. "It wasn't you. Sorry, Blaze. Just got caught up in some shitty memories. I shouldn't be letting old news get to me." Once I straightened my bottoms, I couldn't help but touch her again. I scooped her hand up and laced my fingers through hers. "I have a deal to propose. But hear me out before you shoot it down."

"Oh, Christ, not one of your deals," she complained, trying to pull her hand away.

Her protesting gesture just made me grip on tighter. "This one's all for your benefit, trust me."

She was the one to sigh in resignation this time. "Let's hear it, and I'll judge for myself."

"I think that until we pull into port in Hawaii, there should be nothing but rest and relaxation for you. All day, every day."

"That's not too hard to agree to, Mr. Twombley. What's the catch?"

"Why do you think there's a catch?"

"There's always a catch, Grant. I wasn't born yesterday. A deal, by its very nature, implies that both parties stand to gain or lose something valuable."

"Seriously, there's no catch. These are the reasons I set up this escape plan in the first place. You need time to relax and unwind. Get your head settled. Too much has been going on around you, and I don't think you've stopped long enough to process any of it properly."

She continued to eye me skeptically. "Who gets to determine what properly looks like in my life, other than me?"

"You're right. No one does but you." I grew very still because I knew uttering the next sentence had the potential to be like pulling the pin in a live grenade in this small cabin, all while the door was barricaded closed from the outside. "So when are you going to stop making excuses and do it? You need to work through what happened without all the normal distractions of life to take you off the objective." I turned to face her directly and continued. "Let me be an ear to listen. A shoulder to lean on, or even arms to hold you, while you heal. Let me be here for you, baby."

"I don't need a shoulder to lean on. Thank you though. Or to be held, or to cry it out, or any other happy therapy bullshit you found on Google. I'm fine, Grant. Honestly." She yanked her hand from mine and stood up.

"Can we talk about the day I found you on the floor of your room at Clear Horizons?"

She whirled on me and said flatly, "Pass."

"This is exactly what I'm talking about."

"Wh—"

With a level tone, I cut her off. "You're in denial. How are you going to get better if you don't deal with your problems, Rio?"

"Better? You think I need to get better?" Her voice rose in volume with every word she spoke. "Getting better"—she paused, long enough to shift her weight from one hip to the other—"implies something is wrong in the first place." The same brandy-colored eyes that could entice me now widened with the heat of her temper. "Is that what you think of me, Grant? That I'm some lost, sick, sad soul that needs your healing touch? Christ, you sound so elitist right now. Do you hear yourself?"

"That's not what I meant," I said calmly, hoping like hell my demeanor would affect hers as well. "And that certainly is not the position I'm taking—that I'm better than you."

"The hell it's not! You know what? Mr. Big Shot COO? You can shove your healing vibes up your ass and let them shine like the noontime sun! I would've thought that out of all the people in my life"—she stabbed her index finger right in my face—"you'd be the last motherfucker to judge me!"

With Rio on the verge of hysterics, I stood to—shit—to what? I didn't even know what to do. I cautiously approached as she wore a path in the carpet with her pacing.

Back and forth and then she shouted, "You saw what I went through!"

Back and forth and then another shout, "You've seen the pain I've been in!"

On the next lap, I intercepted her with open arms to hold her close and calm her down. But in perfect Rio fashion, she batted at my outstretched arms when I got near.

"No. No, forget it, Grant. I don't need a savior. I don't need anything—from anyone. My husband dying didn't make you the king of my world! You're neither my conservator nor my fucking liege!" She surveyed me from head to toe and finally, with a calming sigh, said, "I don't understand where you get off exactly, but you can rest assured, it won't be inside of me again." With that conclusive dictate, she left the cabin and soundly slammed the door behind her. A clear signal not to follow her.

I dropped wearily to the bed and started rubbing my throbbing forehead.

This woman would drag me to the edge of sanity right along with her.

It wasn't a matter of *if* anymore.

"Damn it," I muttered.

How the hell had that exchange taken such a wrong turn?

I repeated the scene in my head, picking it apart for where I'd steered wrong. But my replay discovered nothing.

"Damn it," I echoed, growling now.

I'd done nothing wrong. And I sure as hell refused to keep playing along with her I-am-invincible mask, perpetuating the ruse of her mental stability. It wasn't a fleeting concern. I'd stopped her from torching an entire building—twice—for fuck's sake. The second time, there had been people inside the place.

Innocent people.

No, we had to get to the bottom of all this acting out. Even if she never spoke to me again when we made landfall. Of course, that was the last thing I wanted, but we would address the charred elephant in the room, even if it was the last conversation we ever had.

Thinking she probably could use some alone time, and hopefully come to her senses that I wasn't the enemy here, I checked my email. Even though I had posted an away message on my account, there were still a few legitimate issues that needed to be addressed. Before going to find Rio, I called Elijah to check in and see what the general climate around the Shark household was.

"Hey, man," my friend said in greeting.

"How's it going?" I asked, my tone void of energy.

"Well, whatever went down with you and Bas earlier left me with a real hornet's nest around here." He chuckled. Sort of. "So yeah, thanks for that."

"I'm sorry. Honestly, man."

And indeed, I was. But at the same time, I knew if anyone could handle Sebastian's ire, it was Elijah Banks.

I paused for a few beats, hating to start the next topic. "Hey, listen though, when Bas called me, it dawned on me that you and I need to make sure we have our stories straight."

"Stories straight? About what? He knows why you took off with her. Everyone knows you've got it bad for the little firebug."

"Elijah," I growled. "Don't."

"Proving my point perfectly," he said smugly.

"Can we be serious for a minute?" I raked my hair back and continued, "I'm talking about the night of Sean Gibson's accident."

"Oh, right. That."

"Yeah, that. He's not letting this drop. I thought for sure he'd move on to more important things, like...oh, I don't know?" I said sarcastically. "His woman about to drop his spawn?"

"Grant," Elijah said, a slight hint of warning in the one syllable of my name.

"What?" I barked and then instantly felt bad for it. My sour mood wasn't his fault.

My friend's voice softened to the peace-keeper I recognized. "This isn't like you. I know you're spooked about him figuring out it was Rio, but calling his son his spawn? Really? A little much, don't you think?"

"He was such a dick when we spoke earlier, and then Abbi chewed my ear right after. And the storm of a woman I'm dealing with here." I rubbed my throbbing forehead with the pads of my thumbs. "Shit, Elijah. I'm catching hell no matter which way I turn."

"No one ever said playing the hero was easy, my man."

"I'm not hero material, and we both know it," I said dryly. "Anyway, doesn't the hero always get the girl?"

"And gets to wear primary-colored tights!" he said with mock enthusiasm.

"I'll be lucky to get a knee in the balls and a stern lecture."

My buddy burst out laughing at my comment but eventually said, "I always figured it would take a ballbuster like that firecracker to settle you down."

"Whoa there, big man. Who said anything about settling down? She's my friend, and I care about her. I want to help her get over the death of her husband," I protested.

"Over him and under you, I think is what you're trying to say."

Frustrated, I raked my hand through my hair again. I'd be bald by the end of this damn trip if I weren't careful. "For Christ's sake. Why do I have to keep repeating—"

"Cut the shit, Twombley. It's me. One of your best friends. You've totally fucked that woman already; I can feel the possessiveness coming off you in waves. Probably again since you've been stowed away on the high seas if I were a betting man."

"You have no idea what—"

"Yep! Knew it. But for fuck's sake, man. Why is it so hard to admit you're into her? Do yourself a favor and face the feelings you have for her." He paused, and I was seconds from denying his assessment when he finished with, "You'll be in a better place mentally to give her what she needs."

And that was the thing about Elijah Banks that earned

him such a cherished role in my life. He gave it to me straight, whether I wanted to hear it or not. Additionally, with the fucked-up relationship he had had with Hensley Pritchett years ago, he'd gained a ton of insight. The man knew what it took for a couple to stay together, even when circumstances seemed impossible. In the end, he might not have ended up with the girl on his arm, but he sure as hell did everything in his power to try. Elijah was the most emotionally grounded in our friend trio, and I could probably gain a lot of footing with Rio if I listened to his advice.

If I wasn't wasting all my energy doggy paddling in the deep end of my pool of denial.

Concern filled his voice. "You still there?"

"Yeah. Yeah, I'm here. Fuck all this, dude. I can't cope with Bas accusing me of something and then hanging up on me before I had a chance to explain." Then, admitting my more significant concern, "If he drags you into this too? I won't forgive myself."

"Come, come," he tutted mockingly. "Let's not get dramatic. Then we'll all be running around like chickens with our heads cut off. Instead of just Bas." Elijah snickered, and I couldn't fathom why he wasn't taking this seriously. We'd both laid witness while Sebastian Shark obliterated an enemy or two. I never dreamed I'd be on his hit list one day.

"Banks," I said sternly. "Why don't you see the implications here?"

"Oh, I see them. I just don't care." I could picture the careless shrug he gave while he said it. "Bas is going to do what Bas is going to do. We both know that. I swore I would never grovel to the man, and I'm holding to that."

"I have no intention of groveling. I just want to explain

what really happened that night."

"Don't you get it, Grant? He will see the situation the same, no matter what you say. He's already appointed himself judge, jury, and executioner. Just like he always does." Then he scoffed, "I, for one, won't be showing up to his courtroom. Ever."

"But—" I started, but my best friend cut me off.

"No, man, listen to me. I did what I did that night without apology. I was there for one of my best friends when he called me for help. I will never feel guilty about that. Did we cover up some shit we shouldn't have, as far as the law is concerned? Probably. But do I feel remorseful about it? About helping you out? No. I don't. Nor will I, no matter how deeply the almighty Shark sinks in his teeth."

One last attempt to make him see reason. "Elijah—"

But he cut me off again. Damn this guy.

"It's called conviction, Twombley."

Or fucking idiocy. Either or.

"I'll never forgive myself . . ." I said quietly.

"Well, that's on you, then. But you don't have to worry about Bas and me. The man understands that I operate on principle. Always. If he knows I was involved, he can bring it up with me, not take it out on you. Don't be a horse's ass and fall on the sword so easily."

"You really are an amazing friend, Elijah. And an outstanding human being. I'm proud to call you my friend."

"Even if I told you I rode your girl Shawna for three hours straight last night?" he floated past me.

"Fuck you! You did not. You're not her type, not in the least." Strangely, not an ounce of jealousy twisted in my gut, where it usually would have in response to his dig.

"In fact, I did. And Jesus H. Christ, no wonder you tip that woman the way you do." Then he let out a low, tormented groan. "That girl's got kinkier needs than you and me put together."

"Shit," I said, grinning while I remembered my last romp with Lulu's hottie. "Don't I know it." I chuckled. "Was she able to walk today?"

"Not my concern," he said offhandedly. "I'll catch you later, chief. I need to do some legit work today at some point."

"Elijah?" I asked, not sure if he'd already disconnected.

"Yeah?"

"Thanks, man. I mean . . . for everything."

"Catch you later, Twombley," he said.

Elijah Banks was never one to take credit for the good he put back into the world. He'd much rather everyone think he was the dick-swinging playboy he made himself out to be.

I flopped onto my back and stared up at the ceiling. By my calculations, we had at least four days remaining until we arrived at our destination. I had to make peace with my shipmate, and I had a feeling she wasn't going to roll over easily. She never did, so why would she start now? That thought made me grin and then audibly chuckle.

"Oh, Blaze," I said to the walls. "What am I going to do with you?"

After a nice long, hot shower, I dressed for a balmy evening and went to find my girl. Okay, so not my girl, per se, but the one I was currently bending over backward to please . . . all while my mind—and my heart—were in knots. I didn't really know what I planned to say to her when I found her, but I knew when I'd designed the day's meals with the chef that morning, I'd asked that dinner be ready in a half hour from now.

I also knew as I strode down the short passageway that I owed the woman an apology.

Maybe what I'd said earlier was insensitive. Perhaps the way I'd assumed I knew what was best for her was my attempt at playing king, as she so astutely accused. And just maybe, presuming to know what she needed to heal was high-handed.

But she had to realize I was in deep with her, and I couldn't help wanting to make things right in her life. Help her wipe out the pain of losing her husband, and when she was ready... fill that void myself. If she thought I was playing king, was there any chance she would just let down her guard... and be my queen?

At the last cabin door in the corridor, I paused and listened near the door. Rio's soft voice could be heard. Was she singing? I put my ear against the panel and held my breath, really zeroing in on what sounded like a lullaby. As quietly as possible, I tried the polished nickel knob and found it unlocked, so I pushed the door open a few inches.

Rio lay on the bed with her little feline friend asleep on her chest. While she absentmindedly stroked his silky black fur, she sang softly to him. It was precious and gut-wrenching at the same time. Before her husband died, the woman had confided in me that they were desperately trying to have a baby. As Abbigail's due date loomed closer on the horizon, she was probably lamenting her childless, and now husbandless, life.

My quiet knock pulled her from her tune, and she scanned me with her soulful eyes where I stood in the doorway.

"I come in peace," I said, offering the Vulcan salute. The gesture had the desired effect as a coy grin spread across her lips.

"I think you're way too tall and antagonistic to be a Vulcan, Tree. No matter which generation you favor." She giggled. Rio put up her hand to make the foreign greeting's symbol but had to hold her fingers apart with her other hand.

"Fail," I said teasingly. "No true Vulcan involves two hands!" I threw my head back and laughed harder.

"I don't think I'd be Vulcan regardless." She shrugged and sat up taller against the headboard when Robert scampered away from the commotion. "They're much too placid for my temperament."

"Mind if I hang out with you?" I asked, motioning to the bed.

"It's a free country last time I checked."

"Baby, can we stop? I wanted to apologize before dinner. The captain told me he wanted to power down for the night, so I asked the crew to set up our meal on the bow. Does that sound okay?"

"It sounds great. Perfect, actually. Is it warm outside?"

"It is. It's a beautiful night to enjoy the stars. Do you want to shower and change?" I ducked my head to try to read her expression while explaining, "So I can have an idea of timing for the chef." Every question or comment felt like I was walking the plank. One wrong comment, and I'd be swimming for the safety of the shore. This time, maybe literally.

"Yeah, okay." She was thoughtful for a moment and then added, "Actually, that sounds like a great idea. I'd like to wash this day off me."

There was definitely a dig buried in that remark, but I refused to take the bait. We would have a lovely night under the stars if it killed me.

But there was a niggling feeling in the back of my

mind that this woman had the power to do just that. If not physically, then emotionally. I wanted to rediscover the connection we had when we first became friends. Before Sean Gibson died and left this girl's amazing, fiery spirit and lust for life snuffed out like one of the fires she was so fond of starting.

I also knew I couldn't be the only one who wanted to fix things between us. She had to want it too. We both had to make an effort. Just as she reached for the doorknob, I spoke up. "Rio?"

Her shoulders dropped as she let out a sufferable sigh. "What?" she responded tersely but didn't turn to face me.

"Turn and look at me." Unwittingly, my tone shifted into the familiar Dominant timbre I used to ensure I got my way with a woman. It fit like a glove for me, and I had forced myself to forget what it did to the woman standing in front of me. The same woman who now dropped her hand from the latch and slowly turned toward me.

Goddammit, she was breathtaking. Even in her shabby state, she robbed the air right out of my chest, and an unwelcomed pain took its place instead. Shit, what was the right approach with her? I'd never been so turned around where a female was concerned, but she straight up perplexed me.

And thoroughly captivated me.

So I just let whatever I was thinking flow out of my stupid mouth. "Baby." Pain from the depths of my chest changed my tone again. "Can we stop all this? Please."

While I wasn't as stingy with the word as my self-important best friend, Sebastian, I didn't use the term very often.

"All of what, exactly?" Rio volleyed back while looking up to meet my imploring stare with her narrowed, suspicious one.

"Arguing, for starters. I want to enjoy our time away from everyone and everything. Not be at each other's throats the entire trip. Doesn't that sound better? A truce, I guess you could call it."

What I really wanted was to pull her into my chest and bury my nose in her hair. Wanted to feel the warmth of her body pressed against mine and stop denying the attraction we shared.

Rio, on the other hand, looked like she was marching to the gallows. Her face held a full scowl, and I braced for an acidic response. But in the usual fashion, she turned on a dime, relaxed her features, and said, "Sure. That sounds good."

Although I was bewildered—again—I exhaled and tried to let the knot of tension in my gut loosen. "Okay," I sighed, feeling how afraid I was to release the full breath. "Good. I'm glad."

"I'll shower so we don't keep the crew in the galley all night." When she went into our cabin, I continued up to the deck to speak to the chef.

The sun was starting to make its descent on the horizon, and the Pacific was quiet and serene. I pulled in a long breath while leaning on the rail and welcomed the strange sense of comfort that came from staring across the deep amber sunlight that sparkled on the rich cobalt waters.

I was so lost in that personal Zen, the sound of the sliding glass door between the cabin and deck startled me. I pivoted as Rio stepped out and joined me at the rail. Her white cotton sundress picked up the breeze and billowed out like the mainsail of a tall ship.

"Wow, this is really beautiful. Where are we?" she asked.

Nature has nothin' on you, baby.

Completely losing my train of thought watching her tuck her short hair behind her ear, I finally answered, "I have no idea, and I kind of like it. My mind needs a break from worrying, thinking, and tracking details nonstop."

"Understandable." She gave a perfunctory nod. "So, is dinner ready? I'm starving. If nothing else, this trip has taught me how much of a grazer I am."

I twisted my mouth in disapproval but held my tongue. I was the one who just pledged not to argue and knew for sure that anytime her eating habits came up for discussion, she got defensive. Of course, my observant woman instantly noticed the internal struggle I was waging.

"Grant." She put her delicate hand on my arm. "Not everyone needs four full meals a day the way you do." Then she gave me a little smile and said, "Look at the difference in our sizes." She pointedly looked at her hand, resting on my muscular forearm, before continuing. "If I ate the same amount of food you did? Oh my God." She rubbed her forehead in distress. "I'd be as wide as you are tall."

"You're right, you're right." I held my hands up in surrender.

Playfully, she tilted her head and cupped a hand to her ear as though trying to hear a distant sound. "Wait. What did you just say?"

Without thinking, I snatched her by the waist and pulled her close to me. She smelled heavenly and felt even better. In the shower, I'd peered at the label on her body wash and had been intrigued. Was the combination of bitter blood orange and pomegranate that invigorating? Now, inhaling them on her soft skin, I couldn't agree more with the label's promise. Christ, I was the poster child for invigorated at the moment.

I ran the tip of my nose back and forth along the length of her neck until she finally let out a sigh and relaxed in my arms. I had her hoisted off the ground in my embrace like my favorite doll. I wouldn't mind holding her to my chest all night. If only she'd just give in and let me.

"You smell so good. I love that orange on your skin," I growled just below her ear.

She pulled back to look at my face before answering. Mentally I geared up for one of her zingers, but she surprised me with a smile instead. Rio simply said, "Thank you." As I set her back on her feet, she asked, "Are you having a hard time without your usual selection?"

The crew began passing by with large serving trays of food. Rio stretched her neck to follow their progress before asking, "Where are they going?"

"I told you, I thought we'd eat on the bow tonight. Wait till you see the view from up there. Plus, it's much more private than back here, where everyone goes in and out." I motioned to the slider with my chin. "Leave your shoes here, though. It's easier and safer to walk up barefoot."

She looked nervously from the narrow walkway to me. "You go first. Then I'll know where to step. I know you would never let me fall."

If only she saw the truth in her words, we could really start to get somewhere.

CHAPTER SIX

R I O

"That was fantastic. Just one big...fat...problem," I said with a satisfied groan, suppressing the urge to stretch my arms overhead along with it. I'd already broken a number of my mother's etiquette rules in the last hour. She'd be pinching her face in disgust at the moans and hums I'd let escape with each savory bite of our decadent dinner. I snickered at the thought and followed with an actual snort. All it took was thinking of the litter of kittens she'd birth if I gave in and let my arms actually have the long stretch overhead.

A chuckle from the stunning man to my left brought me back to the moment. "What's that, baby?" His grin stayed in place as he waited for my answer. We'd been really enjoying the night, and I knew it was because I'd been so agreeable.

Guilt crept across the tops of my thighs, its icy fingers making me shiver. The unwelcomed emotion had a way of affecting me the exact same way every time. Even the glorious glow of my dinner mate couldn't melt away the awful sensation.

Guilt. What a useless feeling.

I faked a smile to tamp down the demons lurking in the shadows of my heart. It didn't help. They rose up, trying to take over, making it impossible to remember what I was talking about. I still came up empty, making it harder to resist the number one go-to move in my playbook. Verbally victimizing the nearest unsuspecting passerby. But it turned out guilt could serve a purpose after all. In this case, a reminder that not even four hours earlier, I promised myself to go easier on the guy waiting for my reply. He'd turned his life inside out for me, and I'd been nothing but surly and terribly unfair up to this point of our impromptu getaway. That's how I was mentally rebranding it, anyhow. It lent everything a lighter feel, at least—and I vowed that would extend to my bad attitude, as well.

It wasn't too late to correct that course.

"I completely forgot what I was going to say." With a playful thump to the side of my head, I added, "I think I'm in a carb coma from that divine carbonara. Was that not the best ever?"

Grant smiled. Unlike mine, his was genuine—as they usually were. "It was definitely delicious. My guess, though? Yours would be better."

I gave him a skeptical look out of the corner of my eye. "You really don't have to suck up to me, Twombley."

He frowned. "I usually save my sucking skills for other activities, Ms. Gibson."

"Knock it off," I chastised instead. "That dinner was amazing! You can admit it without my ego taking a hit. Trust me."

Grabbing the bottle from the ice bucket, Grant offered, "Let's kick back out here and finish this bottle of champagne under the stars. What do you think?" He stood from his chair at the small dining table and held his hand out to help me do the same. We'd already had more than half the bottle with dinner, and my head was a little fuzzy. The nighttime air was balmy and still, other than the sounds of the sleek hull cutting through the water. We were cruising at a much slower pace than we had in the daylight.

In a quiet, feminine voice that barely sounded like my own, I agreed. Shaped into the fiberglass structure of the boat was a large bed-sized cutout. A striped cushion padded the area, making the spot perfect for sunbathing by day and stargazing by night. Grant helped me get situated on the mattress and then handed me both our champagne flutes before climbing up to join me. When a few crew members came to clear the last of our dishes, Grant asked them to bring us a blanket and another bottle of champagne, and I opened my mouth to protest.

"Just in case. We don't have to open it. But if we decide to indulge, we won't have to go inside."

I sighed and flopped back against the sumptuous pillows that lined what I considered the headboard of this perfect sunbed. Or moon bed—maybe? Why was I even arguing? We didn't have to be at work the next morning. We wouldn't have to drive home, and no one was around for hundreds, maybe thousands, of miles. Wouldn't it be nice—no, amazing—to just let it all go for a while and relax? Exactly like Grant had proposed. When I had allowed myself to really turn it over in the shower that afternoon, I couldn't come up with a logical reason why I was fighting his plan so stubbornly. Maybe it was precisely what my soul needed.

When Grant was finally situated beside me, he let out a long, contemplative breath.

"Penny for your thoughts, Tree."

"Ah, it's nothing," he said dismissively.

"Oh, I'm definitely calling bullshit with a sigh that heavy."
I kept my gaze trained on the glass in my hand, as to not add

extra pressure on him to open up.

"I enjoyed dinner with you." He paused, maybe a few beats too long, but I waited. Eventually, he added, "It felt like it used to between us, and I've missed that. Missed you. I guess I hadn't realized just how much until having it again."

Instead of responding right away, I stared out across the water. The moonlight cast a pale glow throughout the dark sky and equally dark water. There were so many things I wanted to say to this man. Needed to say. Letting my guard down never came naturally to me. Not even with Sean, and I had years to try to get it right with him.

Strangely though, Grant understood me on a level Sean never had. Allowing the cork out of that thought's bottle made me feel terribly disrespectful to my late husband. The more the concept breathed and wafted around the room, the more scared I became about the man sitting beside me. It probably explained why I ran so hot and cold with Grant. I wanted to be close to him. Open up and bare my soul to him. Yet when I did that—in even the smallest degree—it felt like an awful betrayal to my husband. Well, my late husband. I constantly felt like I was being unfaithful to a dead man. And how foolish was that?

Already, I envisioned Sean himself laughing at the absurdity of my worries. Just thinking about how understanding he always had been made me smile.

Right before the tears came.

But stopping them...utterly impossible. They coursed out, unwelcomed and hot, and I immediately pawed at my cheeks to dash them away. Especially before I ruined the special moment between this amazing man and me. This extraordinary human being who was still living and breathing and simply being there for me.

"Hey, hey," Grant crooned, capturing my hands in his version of a comforting move. But I just got more frustrated.

I turned my face into his chest, thinking to hide there while I pulled myself together. Of course, Fate and Irony took turns pointing long, arthritically distorted fingers at me while they laughed. Because I didn't get my shit together. Oh, no. Quite the opposite, in horrific and messy detail. Racking, hitching, hiccupping sobs tore up my throat, escaping with every breath I sucked in and labored out. I didn't just fall apart. I shattered into a million awful shards.

Yet all the while, even as the fragment count climbed into the billions, this gloriously beautiful man rocked me in the strong cocoon of his capable arms. He hushed a gentle litany of kind words to me. Between his sentences were baritone hums and silken whispers, also replete with his steady strength. He was giving it all to me without conditions or caveats or even smartass remarks. He was giving it all to me as if he'd been waiting a lifetime to do so.

My God.

Where had this man come from? I seriously needed to know. More importantly, when heaven finally discovered they were missing one of their angels, would they insist on having him back? Because I wasn't sure about much these days, but I knew one thing with complete certainty. I wouldn't survive losing another man I loved in one lifetime.

Finally—thank God—I settled quietly into the crook of his neck and closed my eyes. I would be a happy girl to fall asleep in his arms, under the moon and stars with the sounds of the Pacific lapping at the underside of the boat in a rhythmic lullaby. Grant seemed equally at peace, and we stayed quiet for a long time. He finally pulled back subtly, I guessed to check if I'd really nodded off, and the slight shift of my weight on his lap made something else obvious between us.

Much. More. Obvious.

I had been so unfair to this handsome, healthy, and virile man. With a lazy smile, I looked up into his gorgeous face. The face with the hopeful blue eyes peering down into mine. We both knew what we had shared the morning before. What we had shared before at my house.

But just as quickly, he looked away, and a stab of insecurity pierced my chest and caused me to avert my eyes too. Grant caught my jaw with his quick hand and with two fingers raised my chin, so I had no choice but to meet his steel-blue gaze in the night.

"I'm trying like hell to be noble here, baby. Don't take it for anything else." His voice was low and lust heavy as it vibrated through his chest and into me where our bodies touched.

"Grant." I sighed. How did I possibly tell him all the things I wanted to say?

"Hmmm?" He nuzzled his nose into my hair just past my ear, and I shivered. "Are you cold? Let's cover with the blanket." He was spreading the thing over us before I could get a word out otherwise, but it did give me an excuse to snuggle into him closer. I wrapped my hand around to the back of his neck and ran my fingers through his hair, trying to work out the right sentiments.

"It really hit me this evening, how unfair I've been to you. Hot one minute. Cold the next. I owe you an apology for that, except, well—shit." I laughed a little girlish laugh—so not like me—making me wince hearing how it sounded when it came out. "Well, an apology doesn't even seem fair either. You've been so good to me—a rock-solid fortress. And I've been a bratty girl throwing fits. I've been rude to you and short-tempered, and—"

I cut in on myself once I found the courage to look up and meet his gaze again. I wasn't planning on that—there were plenty more shortcomings to list—but before I could continue, he smoothly reached out with a couple of fingers, stopping any more words from coming from my lips.

Right before he swept in and covered my mouth with his. Immediately . . . I was lost to him.

The man definitely accepted my apology—while claiming contrition from my lips and tongue with his own. He demanded my remorse from the skin along my jaw, all the way back to my ear with sharp bites and soothing licks, as only he could do. But he didn't stop when he got there—and I didn't want him to. Grant yanked my body beneath his and then loomed over me, powerful and demanding and decadent in his golden glory. With a sensual groan, he kneed my legs apart and settled into the space between them. At the same time, he slid his bent arms under my shoulders to cradle me in his strength and sanctuary.

"Does this mean I'm forgiven?" I asked breathlessly.

"Not yet," he growled. "But you will be by the time we're done here tonight." The promise in his words and the playful gleam in his eyes shone as brightly as the North Star. He was just as much my guiding light in the dark. My direction. My affirmation that everything was going to be okay—and soon, maybe he'd even help me find the way home.

The lights flicked off in the cabin behind us, so we knew the crew had finished their nightly duties and were calling the day complete. They were moving about so early that morning, so they had to be exhausted.

"It's so dark out here," I whispered up to him.

"Don't be afraid."

"I'm not afraid of anything. Not anymore."

"What does that mean?" He ran his fingers over the curves of my brows and then my cheeks, studying every detail of my face while he waited for my answer.

"I don't know." I sighed. "It feels like the worst has already happened. I've already felt the worst pain a woman can feel, apart from losing a child, I suppose. And clearly, that will never be in the cards for me now, so I can put that one up on a shelf somewhere."

Grant's ordinarily bright-blue eyes turned dark with sadness, and I wanted to recall every word I had so selfishly let pass over my lips.

With both hands, I reached up and tugged his thick hair. "Please don't be sad for me. I can't stand that look of pity on your face right now."

"It's not pity, Blaze."

"No? Are you sure?" I pressed, not convinced, and tried so hard to keep the bitterness from my voice.

"It's empathy," he answered and then kissed me once more. "And there's a big difference. I don't want to talk about my shitty childhood right now." He rolled his eyes dramatically toward the moon. "I mean, talk about a hard-on killer, but there's a lot about me you still don't know. So, for now, you'll just have to trust me when I tell you that I know about heartache. I know about survival and how hard it can be to learn to trust love again."

For a few moments, he just stared down at me, and the air was charged with something more intense. Something lusty and primal that was nearly palpable. I felt like a rabbit in the middle of circling, ravenous coyotes. Except I didn't mind being the rabbit in this situation, and there was only one coyote. A very tall, very sexy coyote.

"Blaze," he rasped, stretching his entire body out above mine.

"What?" My voice was needier than I intended, but Grant's next comment quickly took away any concerns about showing all my proverbial cards to the man. Or about anything else.

"I have to be inside you."

Trouble was, I was unable to do anything but stare back at him. Luckily, my body seemed to have the answer though. It took the wheel without input from me or my brain, and I gladly let it. I parted my legs to let him settle there, and slick arousal rushed to my core.

"Such a good girl," Grant rumbled from low in his throat, and the sound resonated in my chest too.

I wanted to protest immediately. The praise that many women fell all over themselves to receive had the exact opposite effect on me. I fought most of my life to be an individual. I didn't need another person's approval of anything I did.

"Stop."

"Stop what?" I whispered.

"The war you're having with yourself over a few simple words."

"I'm not—" I began to explain but stopped the moment Grant sank his teeth into my bottom lip. With his blue eyes boring into my mahogany ones, he kept the pressure on the tender pad until I whimpered.

"I think you're stunning when you hand your body over to me." Finally, he soothed my throbbing lip with a slow swipe of his tongue. "If praising you is part of the process of enjoying it for me, that doesn't change who you are fundamentally."

I continued staring up at him and memorizing the details of his beautiful face. The man had the bone structure of a Greek god and the swagger of a Hollywood A-lister. It didn't go unnoticed how quickly he offered that answer and how polished it sounded when he did. Way back in the corner of my mind, a nagging voice told me this wasn't the first time he'd recited that answer to a woman—and likely wouldn't be the last.

Silently I told that nagging voice to shut the fuck up and let me enjoy myself for a change. Grant must have noticed my shift to acquiescence, because precisely at the moment I decided to let my guard down and scratch the itch that had been building between us again, he covered my mouth with his.

The aggressive, possessive, demanding version of Grant Twombley was present and accounted for. His kiss had equal parts teeth and tongue as it did lips and whispered promises. I wanted to moan and writhe seductively, but all I managed was a feeble whimper of desperate need. Jesus, holy son of God. I knew from my past time spent with him that he was an excellent lover. Fine, he was capable of blowing the roof off with just a clever twist of his hips.

But when we had been together the day before, he had been cautious and measured. I had worried that I would never see this side of him again. Concerned that he would treat me like I was fragile, damaged goods that couldn't handle his Dominant nature. Not only could I handle it, I craved it. And while I struggled with the finer points of the dynamic when he was in this particular frame of mind, I definitely did not desire vanilla sex.

No—I was more of a Rocky Road with sprinkles, whipped cream, and a cherry on top kind of girl. I'd let Grant see a little bit of this side of me once before, but he had yet to see the whole picture of my cravings. Even Sean had never seen this side of me. I'd kept it hidden from him our entire marriage, instinctively knowing he would've never understood my darker fantasies. This part of me that so desperately needed to be satisfied...

But Grant would. In fact, he was one of the few men who would not only understand but could also satisfy my needs.

Just as the thought vanished from my mind, Grant shifted his weight so he could give me a lingering look, from head to toe. "Something just changed in your whole body," he stated, sounding more like an investigator than a high-powered businessman or even a horny playboy.

I twisted my face and looked at him. "Are we role-playing as a detective and suspect right now?"

His grin was contagious as some sort of plan seemed to gain wings in his devious mind. "The idea has merit, Blaze. I probably have a pair of handcuffs in my luggage somewhere."

"I'm game if you are," I said mischievously.

He stood up, never taking his eyes off mine. "Are you okay if I look around in the cabin for a few things? It's pretty dark out here, and I don't want you to freak out."

"I can turn the light on my phone on. Do you need help? Maybe if we both look—"

He held up his hand to interrupt me. "Baby, criminals don't help their interrogators collect supplies they're going to use to torture confessions from them." Grant waggled his brows as he finished his sentence, and a giggle sprang from my lips and echoed out across the water.

"Oh, do you find that funny?" Somehow his voice had become deeper and more menacing, and I snapped my mouth shut so fast, I nearly bit off my tongue.

My new playmate leaned in close—so close, in fact, the tips of our noses brushed each other's. "Now you sit here and come up with a plausible defense. I'll just be a minute." He winked and followed it with a forceful kiss, nipping my bottom lip with his teeth and tugging until I moaned.

When he stepped back, his eyes glittered with mischief and his erection made the front of his pants fit in a deliciously snug way. True to his promise, within a few minutes he was back, surprising me by coming up from behind. I still wasn't completely familiar with the layout of the boat, so I had expected him to return the way he had gone.

Grant climbed back onto the sunbed with me and knelt beside me. "Close your eyes, little criminal," he instructed, and I sat up taller, making a big show of squeezing my eyes shut.

Grant chuckled before saying, "Don't think eagerness is going to get me to go easy on you now, lady. You had your chance to cooperate with the authorities earlier and chose not to. So now, just answer my questions when I ask them. Got it?"

"Fuck you." I popped my eyes open just to glare at him, channeling all the rage I had felt the day we sat in the downtown conference room with the LAPD investigators. "I don't have to do anything without my lawyer present."

"Oh, no." He tsk-tsked and leaned in close again, shifting to the side at the last moment so he could speak right into my ear. The warmth from his breath fanned across my neck and pebbled my skin. "Now, see, I was going to be nice and not blindfold you. But just for that insolent mouth and the daggers you're shooting me . . ." Grant surprised me by sinking his teeth into my ear lobe. Really hard. He finally released the abused pad of flesh when I gasped in pain. "You leave me no choice, miss. Cooperate, and your interrogation will go much smoother. Am I making myself clear?"

"Fuck you," I said brazenly. "How's that for clear, Detective? Do you need me to spell it out for you?"

"All right, we can do this your way." He chuckled. "Now, be still while I slip this on." He fit something over the top of my head and into place, covering my eyes. Instinctively, I reached my hand up to touch what I guessed was similar to a sleep mask. But he stopped my motion with his strong hand. Gripping my wrist, he lowered it back to my lap.

"Let go of me," I said through clenched teeth, trying to pull my arm free and getting nowhere. Oh, this could be so much fun if we weren't on a boat. Nothing like a little game of chase to ramp up the libido.

"That's really too bad, little jailbird," he growled. "You're not calling the shots here." He exhaled a lusty sigh, and I could feel his body weight shift to move behind me on the cushion. "I didn't want to have to do this," he continued his assessment. "But you're definitely a flight risk with all this spunk."

"A what?" I raised my voice a bit, playacting my indignation.

"A flight risk. A runner. Escapee," he explained, and I could picture the smug grin on his face, just by the sound of his voice. What he said next snapped me out of my imagination really quick, though.

"I'm going to restrain you. Don't bother fighting me either, lady. I'm much larger than you. You'll never win. Now kneel up."

With a few quick lashes and buckles, leather wrist cuffs

were in place and then fastened to each other. The snug stiffness of the animal hide bit into my skin, where the bastard had purposefully secured the shackles too tight. A perverse grin played at the corner of my mouth when I realized that somehow this sexy God of a man even knew I'd like that, too.

An air-whistling slap to my ass reminded me to stay in character. I muttered a choice curse word or two under my breath and threatened Grant, "What was that for? I'm going to report you to the warden. You'll never get away with this."

"Bad news, honey. The warden is my brother. He's a bigger bastard than I am. He has cameras all around this place and watches everything that goes on. No one's going to save you."

"You're lying!" I insisted.

I imagined the man shaking his head while he said, "Afraid not. Now, would you rather have an audience watch me eat your pussy or watch you suck my dick?"

"You're giving me a choice?" I scoffed.

"Well, I may be an asshole, baby, but I'm still generous when it comes to fucking fine things like you."

My interrogator stroked a firm hand down my cheek, and I was lost to the rough sensation. When did Grant Twombley do work with his usually manicured hands that he would build up a pad of thick skin on his palms? Or was I that lost between the champagne we drank and the fantasy he was creating with his words and actions that I actually felt what I was imagining?

"Blaze!" His voice was stern when he called my name.

"What?" I snapped but then thought maybe it wasn't the first time he had said it while I was busy daydreaming. And when had he moved in front of me again?

"Watch the tone. You're in no position to be sassing off to me, are you?"

"Do you know what's the best thing about this eye mask?"

"What?"

"You can't tell if I'm rolling my eyes at you."

Apparently, that was the wrong thing to say to the bossy man, because he wrapped his hands under my knees and yanked me until my back was flat on the sunbed. A crazy giggle bubbled up and out of my throat from the surprise movement and left a goofy grin footprint behind where it passed. Dragging my head along the cushion also dislodged the mask so I was able to see my surroundings again.

"You're insane," I said through my smile.

"Possibly," Grant said, but his tone was darker, sounding much more like a threat than my teasing one had. In the span of a breath, I found out why. The pretty sundress I wore became a casualty of his impatience. Instead of unfastening the wrist cuffs and unbuttoning the tiny buttons that made a delicate row through my cleavage, he grabbed the hem and jerked upward, splitting the lightweight cotton in half along the length of my body. I couldn't even protest the destruction of the garment because he was the one who purchased it.

"No! Definitely!" I squealed and regretted it immediately. In a swift move, he took my bound wrists, hoisted them over my head, and hooked them to a cleat on the boat's deck.

"Excuse me, prisoner? How did you remove your blindfold?" He crawled up beside my shoulder while he waited for my answer, knelt up tall once there, and began opening the button and fly on his shorts. I was so mesmerized by his hand dipping into the waistband of his boxers, my mouth went dry, making speech to answer him impossible.

Ruthlessly, he slid a hand between the torn halves of my dress to pluck my nipple. With the hard little point squeezed between his two fingers, he warned, "I'm waiting."

"Graaant," I moaned. "Feels so good." He pinched harder and harder in measured increments, and I let my head loll from side to side while the pain washed over me. Finally, I shouted, "Enough! That's enough." When I went to move my arms from overhead to protect my abused nipple, it was no use. In my stimulated haze, I had forgotten I was still trussed up.

Mischievous blue eyes awaited mine in the dark night. "Where did your blindfold go, Blaze?" he asked with a playful grin that was so sexy and devilish, he could charm every pair of knickers off an entire room of nuns.

"It's your fau—Oohh! Shit! Christ, Grant! Oh my God, yes." I moaned, still trying to catch a full breath from the first nipple pinching when he moved to the other side. We both had dropped the detective and suspect game at that point and were caught up in each other. I realized, probably much too late, how loud my cries of pleasure had been and did my very level best to keep my lips pressed tightly together so another sound couldn't escape. But when he latched on to the same sore bud with his wet, perfect mouth, it didn't matter. Angels were surely singing.

The man looked up over the swells of my breasts to check in with me. "How's that, baby? Feel better now?"

"Grant. Please. Stop teasing."

"Oh, I'm not teasing. Tell me, and it's yours. What do you want? More pain? More pleasure? Both?"

A chain reaction began with the look he gave me. It set off every needy, tingling pulse point between my mouth, which I desperately wanted him to kiss again, and my pussy, which was throbbing and gushing between my thighs.

"Kiss me," I whimpered.

"Kiss you where?" he taunted in response.

"On my mouth. Kiss my mouth, with your lips and tongue," I husked and quickly added, "and don't stop until I say stop."

Grant moved to lie over me, his grin growing wider while he did so. "Don't get carried away now."

"Please," I begged and didn't feel an ounce of shame about it. The man was on me then like a firestorm. Raging flames licked up my body where his hands caressed, leaving trails of scorched, needy skin in their paths. The span of his broad grasp, from thumb to pinky finger, covered more than half my torso in one possessive stroke. When I tried to arch into his palm to guide his ministrations, the bastard just chuckled.

"Baby," he coaxed. "Just relax. You don't have to try to force me into doing what you want. Just feel me on you. Feel me touching you and kissing you." He brushed strands of hair off my forehead and kissed the spot before pulling back to look at me hungrily.

"I need to taste you. It's all I've been thinking about today."

Exactly why was he seeking permission now? Grant Twombley didn't ask for permission in the bedroom. He took what he wanted, and his partners thanked him with standing ovations.

"Please don't let me stop you, Tree," I said, my voice sounding so seductive I barely recognized it. But then... "Grant?" I asked, and he quickly stopped the busywork of moving the halves of my sundress from between my thighs.

His concerned look was like an arrow piercing my heart. A direct hit right through the center and exiting cleanly through the other side. Hastily, I schooled my facial features and choked down the emotions that his one look evoked. Instead, I plastered on my best sexy, sly smile. My expression to match the siren's voice I had just used to invite him to the feast I was serving between my legs. He totally bought the cover-up, too.

"What is it, baby? What's wrong?"

Well, I thought he had.

But I couldn't be bothered with all that at that moment. Messy emotions and all that went with them. Hard pass, thank you very much. I did that once before, and I saw where it got me. I was feeling more and more certain going back there ever again wouldn't be in the cards for me. How much pain could one person endure in their life?

"Can you bring my arms down?" I tried for a demure smile. Not sure how well it would work, but it was worth a try. When Grant just stared back at me, I said, "Please, Grant, my shoulders are getting stiff, and I really want to touch you."

"I'll compromise with you. I'll bring them down to your lap, but not taking the cuffs off," he explained between drugging kisses. My head actually felt like it was spinning when he pulled back to deal with my arms.

In an unexpected move, he swung one leg across my body to straddle my torso. The position put his cargo shorts–covered erection directly in my face. There was no way in hell I was going to miss the opportunity to get naughty with him so close to my mouth, nose, and frankly, every other part of my face I could rub up against him.

A quick assessment and a lot of natural instinct inspired me to reach through his slightly parted legs with my bound forearms and pull him against my face. I nuzzled the bulge in his shorts with my cheek and nose and inhaled the fresh scent of fabric softener. When I looked up to see what the bossy man thought of my behavior, he was watching me with dark, hooded eyes. Slowly, I let my lids drift closed and pressed my lips to the outline of his cock, imagining that it was his skin I could feel beneath my lips and not the thick fabric of his shorts. I crushed him more firmly between my face and my tied hands around back, and he let out an audible groan.

Yes! Finally...

But then he grasped my shoulders and separated our bodies by a few feet. "You're a troublemaker, aren't you?" he asked, trying to look stern but ending his question with a grin on his lips.

I tried to muster a look of disbelief.

"Don't even," Grant rebuked.

"The last thing I was thinking about making while that giant, hard dick was in my face, Grant, was trouble," I guaranteed the man. "Did it feel good? When I was rubbing my face on it, I mean?" Maybe goading him would help break down this wall, or plan, or whatever the hell he had in mind.

"Yes, Blaze. It felt amazing. But I want to finish what I was just getting started. By that, I mean eating your pussy. Then I'm going to put my giant—as you called it—cock in you and ride you until you're begging me to stop. And I may not even then." He leaned down and touched the tip of his nose to mine and said, "So how does that sound?"

"Oh—oh—okay," I stuttered, not knowing how else to respond to his comment.

"Just okay?" He grinned while asking and backing down the sunbed to the end, where he stood.

"Well, no." I sat up a bit, leaning back on bent elbows. "I think that sounds like the best idea I've heard in quite some time. You just have a way of flustering me with the things you say. I'm not used to a man speaking to me the way you do."

"Do you like it, Blaze?" His voice was low and scratchy, and I wanted to rip my own panties off and light a flare down by where he should be instead of where he was standing.

With his stare fixed on mine and his long fingers locked around my ankle, he lifted my leg up to his mouth and kissed the inside of my ankle. The delicate skin was so sensitive, visible goose bumps spread up my entire leg.

"You like that," he commented, not really needing my input.

"Feels so good." I sighed, flopping back down flat. From this position, I wouldn't have to look at his face when I said the next part of what I was thinking. "Grant, please. God, please, here. Just put your mouth on me here." I slid my hands down between my legs and pulled my dress up until it was bunched around my waist. The cool night air washed over my overheated flesh.

"You're trying to kill me. These pale-pink panties are perfect for you. On your milky white skin. You look like you're glowing under the moonlight," Grant said in a low voice.

He positioned himself on the sunbed again, this time between my legs. Nudging my thighs apart to accommodate his body, Grant got comfortable sitting back on his heels and surveyed my entire body.

"Touch yourself while I watch you," he gritted.

"Grant, nooo."

He shot his heated look up to meet mine. "Pardon?" he challenged.

"Seriously. Why are you fucking around so much tonight? Either eat me out or don't. Shit. Now you're just pissing me off. Take these off my wrists. I don't want to do this anymore." I shoved my bound hands in his face.

"Rio," he warned.

"No, I'm fucking serious. There's playing, and then there's going too far. And this is going too far. Free me, or I will find one of the crew members to do it."

In a flash, so many things happened, I couldn't catalog the order of events. Grant grabbed the links that connected the two wrist cuffs and yanked so hard I flew into his lap. I was pretty sure if he hadn't caught me, I would have continued straight over the railing and into the Pacific Ocean. The boat would've kept on cruising, and no one would've even known I was missing . . . maybe ever.

After my body was flush against his and we were both panting, he devoured my mouth so forcefully I thought I might have a fat lip. My barely concealed grin threatened to give away that I was enjoying his roughness.

"Reach between us and pull out my cock," Grant growled against my ear and then bit my neck just below it. His savage moan was swallowed with the kiss I delivered in perfect time with the first tight stroke up and down his shaft. When I looked down between us, the stark difference between his swollen flesh and my feminine grip made the sight even more erotic.

"Shit, girl. So fucking good. Yes! Like that. You know just how I like it, baby."

I stroked him while watching his face contort with ecstasy. "Fuck yes, I do."

But then, in a skillful move, he stood and turned with me in his arms and laid me on my back, exactly in the spot he'd just vacated. The cushion was still warm from his body heat, yet a chill—or maybe a thrill—raced up my spine and made me shiver. The hungry look in his gaze warned of his wicked intentions as he sank to his knees between my parted ones.

Grant reached for the champagne bottle and hoisted the bottle aloft.

"Want some?" he asked with glittering eyes and a naughty grin.

"Mmm, yes, please."

His grin grew wider, and he tilted the bottle to his lips, taking a hefty swig. He crawled up my body and forcefully pressed his mouth to mine, sharing the bubbly alcohol directly from his mouth to mine. I swallowed quickly and looked at him to find a mischievous smile that danced across every feature of his face. His beautiful blue eyes twinkled brighter than the stars, and his cut cheekbones pulled impossibly tighter with his playful expression.

"You're mighty impressed with yourself, I see." I chuckled.

"That was the best champagne I've ever tasted," he growled. "Lie back, baby. I'm still thirsty."

My quizzical look and delay in compliance brought a growl from deep within the man.

"Spread your legs and lie back. Don't make me repeat myself, Blaze."

That damn growl always got the best of me, and as much as I tried to keep my features neutral, the rush of wetness between my legs could not be hidden. Especially after I eased back, both nervous and excited, and shoved that part of myself right into his face.

Grant pulled the damp fabric of my panties to the side and took a good look at the state of my aroused pussy. While making quick work of pulling my panties down over my hips and off completely, he said, "Oh baby, this can't feel good right now." Even though he said the comment with what sounded like sincerity, I'd been in bed with this man before and knew he loved to tease and taunt before giving me what I needed most. Maybe if I just agreed with him, he'd cut to the chase.

"You're right," I whimpered. "I need you. Please."

He moved in even closer, so when he spoke, I felt his words as much as heard them. "Yeah, you do. Right here would probably take care of that ache." As he traced my folds with his index finger, his groan joined my moan in a lusty chorus. With my head tilted back, I tried to focus on the starry sky. If I caught sight of a shooting star, I'd wish for his mouth to make contact with my pussy. Immediately.

While I'd been looking heavenward, Grant had grabbed the champagne bottle and regained my attention by pouring some directly on my sex. I yelped, and he quickly began lapping the liquid off my sensitive flesh, concentrating most of his skill on the pert button at the center.

"Jesus, Grant. God, yes, so good," I praised and weaved all ten fingers through his thick waves since both wrists were still cuffed together.

"Okay, this is the best champagne I've ever tasted. No contest."

I thought for precisely two and a half seconds about how sticky I'd be when we were done, but the moment his mouth made contact with my mound again, I couldn't find the good sense to care about any of it. His skillful tongue and long, talented fingers had me on the verge of climax so quickly the sensation frightened me. I'd spent the last hour in such an aroused state that all it would take would be a final move exactly like the one he delivered next.

"Grant! Fuck, yes! Ooooohh, shit. Shit! Stop! Stop, I can't take any—"

"Of course, you can, Blaze. Fuck, you're so sexy when

you come." The man continued pumping his fingers into me in a slow, lazy rhythm that seemed to draw out the very last molecule of air from my lungs, beat from my heart, and coherent thought from my mind.

When my climax was complete, the sated smile that spread across my lips started a warm glow down to my toes. I had no energy left for hiding it. If my satisfaction fed his ego, then so be it. He deserved the accolades, all of them.

Because something about my orgasm... It had been different this time. Shockingly so.

While the physical release was damn fine, there was more to it than that. A layer of profound beauty...of restorative healing. From exactly what, I didn't know. I was only certain about the damn tears that pricked the backs of my eyes now. Forget about whether I wanted any part of the emotional deluge. A storm of feelings was rolling in, and it wouldn't matter what kind of equipment I had in place to protect myself—or Grant—from the fallout. The damage would be felt across our landscape, and all I could keep hoping was that this amazing, caring, and endlessly giving man would have the staying power to rebuild with me, time and time again.

CHAPTER SEVEN

GRANT

In our cabin's hot shower, I spent long minutes tending to every inch of my flame's beautiful skin. My own body received a cursory suds-and-rinse while I watched her weave precariously on her exhausted legs. As soon as I could towel her off, I helped her into bed. If we were back in Los Angeles, I would've treated her to the complete experience I'd fantasized about. The "You're My Queen" handling that entailed me carrying her to the bedroom and laying her down on my oversize mattress and restarting my efforts to ravage her.

My unsatisfied lust brought me back to the woman before me. Christ, she was captivating. Every breathy sigh she exhaled, interspersed with whispered gratitude, was a new taunt to my oversensitized flesh. Just like that, my desire for this stunning, sexy creature spiked even higher.

Simply put, I needed to come. Badly.

I made sure our door was locked and turned out the lights. Carefully feeling my way along the unfamiliar furniture, I moved cautiously until I found the bed.

"You warm enough, Blaze?" Of course the concern was real, but it was also a damn good distraction for a moment or two. I was in no condition to carry on a full chat, but focusing on Rio accomplished the miracle it always had. I was calmer and steadier because of it.

A sleepy hum was the only response that came from under the covers. The sound, so guileless and adorable, made me smile.

"I wore you out, didn't I?" I chuckled as I settled in beside her. Since I'd put her into bed without bothering with pajamas, I dropped my towel at the bedside. Now, our skin-to-skin contact made my dick jolt with fresh fervor. Goddamn, she felt good, so silky and soft. She smelled even better, the familiar scent of her fresh hair and skin filling my senses.

But I would bet an orgasm she tasted even better.

Fuuuck. I needed to find a way between her lips—either pair would do—immediately.

I slid my arm under her waist and pulled her beneath me, though I didn't let our bodies touch. In my deepest, darkest voice, I growled right against the shell of her ear. "Rio. Katrina. You are the most exquisite little firestorm I've ever laid my eyes on."

I knew she was grinning without pulling back to look. The muscles in her face stretched with her delight.

"It's the truth," I vowed. "I could've stayed in that shower for hours just petting and praising you."

"Well, then, I'll pencil you in for when we make landfall." Though her voice was still sleepy, a sultry edge accompanied her ending sigh.

"It's a deal," I said and let more of my weight settle onto her. I needed to feel every inch of her under me. Over me. Around me.

Fuck, somewhere. Anywhere.

No. That wasn't right. I knew exactly where I needed to be. I had to be inside her. End of the goddamned debate.

There was no way I'd make it through another night of watching her sleep while I did the noble thing and kept my dick to myself. It nearly killed me the first time, so two in a row would mean certain death. In essence, this wasn't even a matter of seduction anymore—it was a matter of survival.

"Grant—" she said, her voice edging toward a protest.

"Open your legs, beautiful," I interrupted in a firm command, "so I don't crush you."

"But—"

"Woman, do you feel this hard-on?" I rolled my hips into her, refusing to be thwarted. At least not easily, anyway.

Rio grinned before saying, "Oh, I feel it. I'd have to be dead not to."

"So? Help a desperate guy out here?"

Another light, captivating laugh—right before she parted her luscious thighs. But before I could release half a groan of approval, she surprised me in one of the best ways imaginable. She hooked her magnificent legs around my hips—but didn't stop there. Quickly, she had her heels pressed into my ass, pulling me closer with an unspoken demand of her own.

I was officially in heaven. Her new position opened her intoxicating pussy to my hard length like a welcome home embrace. Warm—fuck, so warm—and inviting, it took every shred of my self-control not to just drive into her. But her body needed a little more preparation, and that was just fine with me. Maybe better than fine.

Absolutely better.

I dipped in and kissed her. Quietly and carefully at first, starting with her naturally crimson lips before trailing to one side of her mouth. She sighed softly, a perfect encouragement, so I continued my path of affection up over her nose, along one of her pronounced cheekbones, and then back to her perfect ear. Once there, I nipped at the delicious shell, waiting for her next gorgeous sigh as my wordless inspiration.

And maybe those kisses were doing some inspiring of their own, because a low belly moan worked its way out of her, and she dug her heels into my backside even harder. The leverage allowed her to lift her hips off the mattress and create delicious friction against my shaft with her now very wet pussy.

In a husky tone, I moaned, "Oh, yeah, Blaze. That's it, baby. Use my cock for whatever you need, girl." Then panted, "It's all yours. Whatever you want—it's yours—as long as you don't stop doing that."

"Oh, God, Grant." A sigh. "Feels so good." A moan. "I could come like this." A promise? More like a threat.

"No, not this time. If I don't come, I'm going to go blind, I swear. Let me inside that tight pussy."

When she didn't yield to my need, I gave her waist a demanding pinch. Immediately, she released the leg lock she had on my hips. At the same time, her dreamy stare fell to my groin.

And that sure as fuck did it.

No seduction could ever be as perfect as this woman's wide stare. The way she was cataloging every hill and valley of my body as I held my cock in hand and lined up to claim her was nearly as incredible as claiming her itself. The hitch in her breath was like the strike of a match. I was hard; she was hot. I was swollen; she was ready.

After slicking through her arousal to ease the glide, I pushed my way into her. Then again. And again. Just as quickly and thoroughly, I leaned forward to swallow her outcry with an openmouthed kiss.

After a few deep thrusts, my orgasm was building like a wildfire. A spark of need gathered strength, quickly building into a flare of desire that swelled with blinding purpose. The tempo of our passion was so remarkable, it was difficult to comprehend its magnitude until it was almost too late.

Almost.

Through no small miracle, I gathered enough fortitude to freeze midstroke. Rio jolted her stare back up at me. The passion and heat burning on her face were like gasoline to my open flame of desire. Yet I persisted, trying desperately to still her. Just for a few more minutes...

Uh-uh. Nope. I'd be lucky to make it another few seconds.

"What?" Rio demanded, searching me with curious and concerned eyes. "What is it? Grant? Do you want to switch?"

She squirmed, clearly intent on moving from beneath me, but her tiny undulations were torturous quakes of stimulation, drenching my helpless cock. Just like that, instinct and impulse took over. Before I could think twice, I shot my large hand out. I had to stop her wriggling, right the fuck now, and I did—by spreading my broad palm across her throat.

Her eyes bugged, impossibly big.

My dick throbbed, unignorably taunted.

And my mission for self-control? On the brink of utterly ambushed—especially as my sights riveted to where my hand still sprawled across her delicate neck. And then her not-so-frightened stare. And her shallow, sharp breaths from that slightly parted mouth...

Fuck. Me.

"Stay. Still," I gritted through clenched teeth as she watched my personal battle with fascination. "Trying to last,"

I panted out and squeezed my eyes closed for a couple of seconds. I couldn't endure for much longer. For now, I had to shut out the erotic vision I had just created for myself.

But my ordeal continued as soon as I reopened my gaze. The little minx was determined to rob me of my sanity, because she was waiting to make direct eye contact again. Once we did, she mouthed one word to me.

Harder.

I almost gave her a double take. Had she really just...

Oh, hell yes, she had.

And Rio proved as much with her follow-up. The woman blew the doors off my mental brick house by lightly placing her hand on top of mine. The exact hand still clutched around the slender column of her throat.

Well, that was all it took. That one gorgeous gesture. With one silent word, she'd stoked the flame to a full, phenomenal blaze.

Though if I were honest, the fire that burned inside me for this intriguing, infuriating, captivating woman...had a new ground zero. My hot interest for the sassy, sexy little imp beneath me had started months ago, where most heat does in my world—in my dick. But over the days, and through the harrowing experiences she'd endured, feelings sneaked their way up through my body and now simmered in the center of my chest. In my heart. And Rio fanned the emotion with every breath she took. I could openly admit now, those feelings had been building from the moment I met her. And ever since I'd been inside her scorching hot body? My feelings were careening toward alarming. The clanging five-bells-and-a-scream kind.

I never wanted the fire drill to end.

Especially now, as I flexed my fingers to add more pressure to her neck instead of her windpipe. At the same time, I thrust my hips forward.

"Put your hands on the pillow above your head, Blaze. Both of them. Now," I growled. With a deeper groan, I watched her nostrils flare. I reveled in the feel of her pulse that thundered through her carotid, tripling in time beneath my commanding touch.

"Nice," I praised. "Very nice, baby. Breathe and let me do what I want to this tight little body."

My pelvis smacked against her, and I taunted my girl with each thrust. "Does that feel good? Can you feel me deep inside you?"

"Yes. Grant! God, yes!"

"Are you going to come for me again, Rio?"

"I don't … I don't …"

"Is that a yes?" I goaded with a wide grin. As she fumbled for an answer, I released her from my grasp. Just as quickly, I flipped her over to her stomach. She let out a sound, a delicious mix of a whimper and a moan, as I snaked an arm under her, hoisting her ass up to meet my downward thrust. As we rejoined, I meshed my groan with her loud cry. Her pussy was so slick, I slid all the way into her heavenly body in one aggressive motion.

"Fuck! Grant!"

"So good, baby. Christ, you're always so wet for me."

"Mmmm."

She was back to the half moan, and it had never sounded better with the blood that hammered my ears. But it didn't match the stuff filling my dick as she propped herself up on her forearms and looked back over her shoulder to watch me fuck her. Goddamn. Of all the ways I'd envisioned dying, keeling over from an arousal overdose didn't crack the top hundred. But this threat was gloriously real, and I didn't give a single flying fuck—especially as I drank in the glory of Rio pushing back into every one of my forceful strokes. Oh, hell yes—I was so close—and it was so perfect.

Until her whiskey-colored eyes fluttered closed. Oh, hell no!

"Look at me, Blaze. It's now or never, girl. I can't hold back. Come with me, baby." I encouraged her with words and then spanked her ass over and over until the sounds of our slapping flesh and her cries of passion mingled together in a chorus so sweet, I wanted to record the whole thing and save it for my phone's ringtone.

I groaned low in my throat while semen spurted from my cock. I continued to jerk and throb inside her channel even as she expelled an exhausted sigh and surrendered her whole weight into my hands. Supporting her petite frame wasn't an issue. Refraining from using the moment as a great teaching lesson? Not so easy. Because if she would let me help with other things just as easily . . . like her heartaches and struggles and pain . . .

But we'd already been there. A hundred times now. She'd have to connect the dots to the conclusion on her own—if it were to happen at all.

After I was sure I had emptied every last drop I had into her, I eased her down onto the bed and rolled off to her side. She nestled into my open arms, and I pulled the covers over us, and we were lost to sleep.

★ ★ ★

By the time I woke the next morning, the space beside me was empty. I strained to hear the shower running, but no luck there either. Disappointment set in, and I wanted to kick myself for thinking I'd finally made progress with the woman.

I ran my hands over the whisker growth on my cheeks and across my jaw. I was an idiot to think that a pretty moon, a sky full of stars, and a couple of orgasms—even if they were epic— would actually make headway in deciphering this woman's code.

Rio wasn't like any of the other women I'd taken to bed before. Not even close. I was so far out of my league with her. Strange and heavy feelings were sitting right in the center of my chest, making it difficult to breathe.

Shit. Maybe I was just coming down with something. That wasn't a great theory either. Not now, when the best part of our trip was still ahead of us. The Aloha State. I'd made reservations at all the best restaurants in Honolulu and even planned a spa day for Rio at the island's most renowned resort. We would be staying at the luxury complex for one of the nights while the crew cleaned and replenished the yacht before we made our journey back to California.

Today, I thought I'd check out a few more activity ideas— after getting Rio's input, of course. The thought made me laugh out loud. It was like I'd been abducted by aliens in my sleep. Checking out activities? And I wasn't using the word combination as a witty, covert euphemism for *fucking* in front of a G-rated audience. No wonder I was feeling so confused. All this shit was really starting to sound like a relationship, and God fucking knew I had no experience in that department. The closest I'd come to having a relationship with a woman was knowing how she took her morning coffee while I called a car to drive her off my property in the quickest, tidiest manner.

But that was just it. I wanted to do more than navigate a morning after with this amazing, confusing, creative creature. I wanted to linger in bed and drink our coffee from the same cup. I wanted to feel her hair tickle my chin while she snuggled in my arms and we checked our morning emails. I wanted to roll her onto her back and sink into her for a lazy morning fuck session and then take a long hot shower together before we set off to work. Then meet back at home after a long day at the office to do it all over again.

I didn't know what it was about Rio Gibson that had me thinking in a way that was one hundred eighty degrees from the way I usually did. But, well, here I was. Doing just that.

A conviction that, in the next moment, got soldered to my brain—in the form of the woman's own silky voice, drifting through the cabin door.

"Come on, big boy." Her sigh, while exasperated, was an ideal addition to the sweet feathers of her tone. "Don't be like that." Another perfect sigh and then a curiously long pause. "You're much braver than this, Robert. I know you are."

Aaahhh, that explained where she'd gotten off to so early this morning. Although, when I looked at the clock on the nightstand, it wasn't really that early. Last I'd checked, we'd finally stopped fucking around two. The fact that it was now nine wasn't really that out of line.

My stomach growled its embarrassingly loud opinion on the matter, and I thought as soon as my morning erection subsided, I'd be able to get out of bed and focus fully on food.

"Robert! Silly cat! No, come this way, crazy boy."

Well, there was a nice, full incentive—and a perfect piece

of inspiration. With Rio's lush voice trickling in through the walls, I rolled out of bed, padded to the bathroom, and cranked the shower all the way to "H."

As soon as I stepped under the water spray, I gave in to the sweet sorcery of her muffled voice—and mixed it with the magic of my memories from last night.

Instantly, my morning wood was fueled into full arousal. It got even better with a generous amount of body wash, as I roughly worked my cock with one hand and my balls with the other.

"Fuck yes," I croaked, thumping my head back against the shower enclosure. Steam billowed around the cramped space and quickly created a sultry atmosphere in the poorly ventilated bathroom.

I fantasized that my hands were Rio's, and instead of the tentative, feminine grasp she normally used, she handled my dick in the rough, aggressive manner I preferred. It was fucking amazing.

That's right, girl. You know just what I need.

I pictured her staring back at me with her expressive eyes. Sometimes completely wild, sometimes curious and cautious.

Of course, you can suck me, baby. It's all for you, but only if you take it all without gagging, sweetheart.

Christ, the look I'd get after a comment like that. But that was exactly the point, since her array of expressions had the same wicked effect as her actual mouth around my erection. But I'd want more . . . so I'd taunt her more.

Look at me, girl. Uh-oh, I see someone forgot their tear-proof mascara today. And why do these black streaks running down your perfect, pale cheeks make me want to come, Blaze?

I had absolutely no interest in drawing out my pleasure.

My orgasm was going to hit like an unexpected traffic accident. Hard and violent. And no matter what I did to try to change course, I couldn't stop it.

You are so fucking perfect. No . . .

And then I must have groaned aloud, in real time to match the one in my imagination because the sound that bounced around the small shower stall actually startled me that I chuckled.

I'm not going to fuck you today, baby. All you get is my dick down your throat. Yesssss! Squeeze my balls while you do that. Naughty girl. Look at you, perfectly naughty girl. I fucking love this perfect mouth . . . this perfect cunt. Touch yourself for me. Oh, hell yes. Yes! Yes, baby! I love everything about you, girl. I just—

" . . . love you."

I stopped suddenly. But not for long. As soon as the words—those crazy, unthinkable words—hit the air they bounced around the small stall like a bullet in an old, empty steel drum.

But they weren't errors.

Not by a goddamned long shot.

The mantra repeated in my mind as I rubbed out the orgasm with furious pumps and a couple of guttural groans. It didn't take long to milk myself dry. It never did when my gorgeous Blaze was the star of my private peep show.

My eyes were squeezed shut so tight, I saw a rainbow of pinpoint lights dance across the backs of my eyelids when I snapped out of my fantasy. My neck had a terrible cramp on one side, but the orgasm felt so fucking good, it was completely worth it. I was a Rio Gibson junkie and had no interest in getting sober.

Or so I told myself before reaching for my shampoo on the ledge of the shower stall. And lifting my gaze to where Rio stood, framed by the bathroom doorway.

Holy mother of God.

"Rio."

"Grant?" Though her tone was reasonably light, swatches of light and dark pink were scattered across her face. Was she horrified? Aroused? Both? If so, what was that ratio? What the hell was she feeling? Thinking? Concluding?

"How long have you been standing there?" More exigently, how much of the damn fantasy did I actually say out loud? Had I really mentioned I loved her?

No. Of course not. If I had, she'd have already high-tailed it out of the bathroom, the cabin, and off the damn boat. If anyone could walk on fucking water all the way back to California, it was this intrepid fireball—but she seemed content to push a toe at a few tiny puddles on the floor as she remained right where she was, eyeing me like an impish voyeur.

At last she offered, "That's some impressive wrist and forearm action you have there, Twombley." She jerked her chin in my direction while not moving from the doorway.

"Why didn't you say something? Then I wouldn't have had to handle it myself."

"And miss that display of epic sexual prowess?" She shook her head back and forth slowly. "No way."

I was still baffled as fuck—but I refused to endure it dripping wet. I shut the water off abruptly and snapped the towel off the top of the shower stall. Rio jumped back at the cracking sound the cotton sheet made when I shook it out before wrapping it around my waist. I flung the stall door open and didn't pause to drip dry on the bathmat. My intention was way more important.

I stalked straight for her, not stopping until I backed her up all the way across the room and the backs of her knees hit the bed. The momentum caused her balance to fail. As she began to topple, she reached for my forearm for purchase. But I used the moment to twist at the waist, meaning she grabbed at thin air. Her butt hit the mattress with a *thump,* and I leaned in above her.

"Blaze." I growled her nickname and held her brandy stare with the thunderstorm version of mine. "Do you need a demonstration of my—oh, how did you just describe it? Sexual prowess? I'd be happy to stay right here in this bed, Rio. All. Day. Long. And show you just how epic my prowess can be. Over. And over. And over."

With each enunciated word during that finish, I invaded her personal space with more and more force. By the time I finished my threat—or promise, depending on which end of the conversation was winning here—she was flat on her back, and I was once more on top of her.

Funny how we kept ending up in this position.

With one hand, I cuffed her wrists high above her head and circled my towel-covered erection into her core. Instinct and need seemed to drive her actions, though. Her glassy-eyed stare and rich, throaty moan antagonized my aggressive behavior even further.

"Christ, you're killing me," I said. "I could go again. Right now."

"Well? What are you waiting for? The Blue Angels to fly overhead and sky write an invitation for you?"

Holy shit. What I wouldn't give for a chance to go at this sassy girl's ass with a proper wooden paddle. And there was a damn troubling revelation. The challenge in her comeback was tempting a side of me she hadn't made contact with yet. I wasn't sure she was ready now, either.

No. That was more bullshit. I really was sure. She absolutely wasn't ready.

Nor was she as ramped up as I'd given myself credit for. I sank my teeth into her breast, right through the T-shirt and bra she had put on for the day, and she yelped in surprise, though the cry was quickly replaced by a guttural sound of pleasure. The same way I flipped my mien back to efficiency mode.

"Let's go have some breakfast. I'm starving."

"Grant—" she gasped. I'd expected that part. I just hadn't expected her to be so flustered. "Are you serious?"

"Of course I am. You know I don't joke about food, woman."

"Not that, damn it." She huffed. "Are you really going to just leave me like this?"

"Like what?" I tried to play dumb but ended up grinning instead as soon as she growled and flung a pillow at me. It hit me in the ass as I walked across the room to pull out some clean clothes for the day.

★ ★ ★

We decided to eat breakfast on the aft deck. During the meal, a stunning repast with Polynesian omelets as the central entrée, we talked with the boat's captain about how much longer he thought our journey would take. The man told us that if sea conditions stayed favorable, we would be in Honolulu in a day and a half. In short, we were right on schedule.

In return for the captain's update, I gave him a pleased nod. Rio's reaction was drastically different. As the conversation went on, she continued dropping her stare to her plate, becoming fascinated with the scraps of scrambled eggs. By the time the guy walked away, she didn't even notice.

Well, shit.

What was it now? Or what wasn't it? Despite what she blatantly assumed about my mind-reading skills, they weren't all that—especially when she flipped temperatures like this for no apparent reason.

"Are you still hungry?" I finally asked. "Do you want some more fruit, maybe?" But her stretch of silence highlighted how completely she had withdrawn. "Blaze?" I tried again.

After a few more moments, she looked across the small table and met my waiting stare. Okay, so she definitely wasn't mad. But shit, I'd seen that fiery glare enough times to recognize it. On the other hand, there weren't any unshed tears in her eyes, so I wasn't automatically guessing sadness had settled in, either.

"Do you want to tell me what's going on, or do I have to keep guessing?" I queried.

"Oh, but I thought the wise and ever perceptive Grant Twombley knew everything," she bit back.

"That's not fair, damn it," I spat. "And you know it."

"Do I?"

Goddammit.

I barely kept that one silent. Instead I fumed out a harsh breath before demanding, "Why are you saying this? And why the fuck are you acting this way toward me? I haven't done anything. Or have I and just haven't realized it yet? Is this about me cutting things short back in the stateroom?"

Rio gave her head a little shake, grinning as if contemplating a response but then thinking better of it. "No," she finally murmured. "This isn't about that. And I really don't want to fight about it, okay?"

"Fine." I gathered a fistful of my hair. "I mean, okay. That's okay, baby. I don't want to bicker, either. I'm sorry I lost my temper. I don't want to make you upset. I just want to understand what's going on. Will you help me?"

More of the deafening silence. Thank fuck for the constant drone of the vessel's motor, along with the sweeps of water against the hull. I was doing everything in my power to stay calm, and the steady rhythms were a big help—especially as she stared back at me with what looked like solid contempt.

But why?

I couldn't figure anything out...

I took a healthy gulp of water from my glass but kept my stare trained on her over the brim the entire time. She merely closed her eyes and tilted her face up to the morning sun. It was definitely going to be a warm day out on the open water.

"Are you disappointed we're making port soon? Is that what set you off?" I asked it as gently as I could, trying to restart a conversation.

"Set me off?" She dropped her head, now squinting to focus on me. "Don't be ridiculous, Tree. I don't want to be cooped up with you any longer than I have to be."

I decided to ignore that. No point being derailed by her bratty behavior. I was starting to figure out her game. At least I hoped. "Well, I'm just using some logical deduction," I explained. "That is when you did the one-eighty. Mood wise, I mean."

She huffed and crossed her arms. "See what I mean? You

have it all figured out, don't you?"

She clearly wasn't pausing to think about her actions, so neither did I. Without thinking it through at all, I stretched out my arm, snatched the base of her chair, and dragged it across the deck until she was right in front of me. Before she could react, I quickly bracketed her legs on either side with my own. Perfect. I had her trapped in place. And it was exactly as I intended.

"What do you think you're doing?" she seethed and squirmed impatiently.

"Keeping you right here so we can talk this out," I said, countering with calmness. Maybe if I infused the air around us with enough tranquility, it would bring her anxiety down a few notches. But not right away. Rio huffed through her nose like a little angry bull, and I chuckled at the image. Of course, that only served to piss her off more, and she tried to push back from the confinement I'd created with our chairs.

"Damn it, Grant! Let me go!"

I shook my head slowly from left to right. "I don't think I can do that, Blaze."

Not now. Maybe ever.

But I knew better than to say that aloud. Not if I didn't want the woman diving overboard. She'd do it too. Anything to save herself from dealing with the growing emotions between us.

Plus, I had to face a bigger truth than that.

I was being a fool. An unfair one, at that. It was wrong to pin her down and define her feelings for me at this point. What we had—if we had anything at all by now—was still new and fragile and wild and uncertain.

I knew that.

I swore I knew that, and I told myself that over and over. Preached it to myself, really. Yet, somehow, she kept crawling deeper under my skin.

Who the hell was I kidding with that shit, too? She wasn't under my skin. She had penetrated so much deeper than that. Rio Gibson had burrowed a tunnel straight into my heart, and I was so fucked because of it.

Because I wasn't sure how I was going to get her out at this point.

What was making the whole situation worse? There wasn't a single part of me that wanted to.

CHAPTER EIGHT

RIO

Third time's the charm, right? Or so I told myself when my phone vibrated on the bed beside me. I'd ignored it the other two times but figured I had better check the screen in the odd event it wasn't my shipmate. Abbigail was due to labor my nephew into the world any day, after all, and while I didn't hold out much hope of getting a cell signal in the middle of the Pacific Ocean, Grant wasn't the only persistent one around here. He'd said we would be pulling into port tomorrow, so we had to be getting closer to land.

That being said, I wasn't optimistic about being on the shortlist of people Abbi would be calling on her way to the hospital. Not after everything that had happened between her husband and me. But I was still the widow of her brother. Nothing would ever change that. I would forever be her baby's auntie. Before Sean's accident, I'd been a welcomed member of the crew looking forward to Kaisan's birth.

And there it was.

I felt the same familiar weight on my chest whenever the tragic topic came up. Whether it had been voiced aloud or just bounced around in my own head—the feeling was there all the same. Cold. Relentless. Unchanging. Unforgiving. It was just like the lump that rose up in my throat and the chaos that clamored in my mind.

Sean's accident. My husband's death.

So here I sat, the widow of a virile, exuberant, smart, and witty man. The man I adored with my whole heart. But all the love and commitment in the world wouldn't change the fact that he was ripped from my life one weekday afternoon—at three seventeen, to be exact. The time was branded on my memory forever.

Even now, months after the funeral and packing his clothes in boxes for charitable donations, one painful truth stood out among the others. While I was trying so hard to pick up the shattered pieces of my life, the people around me who professed to care the most didn't notice I was dying too.

None of them except for Grant.

The man noticed everything. Every. Thing. He had a way of seeing through the mask and bullshit I sold to everyone else.

Most of my friends and family were so wrapped up in their own lives, they didn't pay attention to mine. And I couldn't really fault them for it. If I were honest with myself, I would have probably done the exact same thing to someone if they were silently screaming for help. It was easy to overlook someone else's pain when your head was buried in the sand of your own daily grind.

But again, enter Grant Twombley. Always the anomaly. He had been the one to offer a steady hand when I needed it. The problem now, I'd gotten used to leaning on him—and it felt too good. Too right. But what did that say about me? My husband died just a few months ago, and I could already see us sharing laughs over pizza and Sunday afternoon movies.

Spending time with Grant was so effortless. He made everything in the world seem right again. Something about his easygoing smile and calm aura made me feel like I could muster the courage to take on the world again. The voyage across the ocean made me see things clearer, and I was pretty sure that was part of his plan the entire time.

My phone vibrated again, and I jumped when I realized I never answered the last text like I had meant to. I read the message on the screen and smiled a small smile. At least I could allow myself to do that when I was locked away with Robert. He wouldn't tell anyone my secret. I just needed to pull my shit together and leave my little hideout and go back to our cabin. There was no way I could fall back into bed with the man, though.

But there was also no way I could keep letting myself fall deeper for him emotionally, either. One of us was going to get hurt, and I knew my heart couldn't withstand any more pain. That tattered organ had battle wounds as though it had been on the front lines of a war with no weapon for defense and no armor for protection. Grant didn't deserve that kind of pain either. Shit, he had been nothing short of accommodating, doting, and amazing. The model good-looking playboy millionaire deserved someone better than me and my laundry list of eccentricities. And that was the nice way of putting it. In a crueler mood, I'd have used terms like *volatile*, *irrational*, and *insane*.

Tough words for the tough love I was trying to impress upon myself. It didn't feel any better than it sounded. Grant would like it even less.

But the matter was settled. It was time for me to put on a mask of indifference and, from now on, resist the sexy charms of the magnificent Mr. Twombley. We were nearly to Honolulu and would have a few days on land in Hawaii before we started the return leg home. I'd be able to get through it all if I kept up the personal pep talks and also avoided any skin-to-skin contact with the man. Or so I'd have to keep telling myself.

I sighed, gave my sweet Robert one last scratch under his chin, and rolled off the bed. I gave my hair a quick finger comb in the helm-shaped mirror on the wall and then was off to find out what was so important that Mr. Twombley was texting me like a teenager with his first phone.

The boat had been providing a sense of safety I'd quickly gotten used to, so I walked with carefree ease through the passageways. The mental security likely came from the defined physical space and the fact that no new passengers had come on board or gone ashore since we left Los Angeles. Whatever the reason, I would definitely miss it when we arrived in Hawaii. My mind rarely found a safe haven from anxious thoughts, bitter memories, or guilt-laden recriminations. For a person like me, the biggest pitfall of spending too much time with her own thoughts often were those very thoughts themselves.

"There you are," he said, sitting up from where he lounged against the headboard, tapping away on his laptop. I didn't miss the way his shirtless torso and trim waist looked in the track pants slung low around his hips. Nope. Not one single inch.

"Here I am," I responded in the same bright tone, darting my eyes around the room. Looking anywhere but back at his graceful body and effortless gorgeousness.

"I was trying to get hold of you."

"I got your texts. I was giving the kitty boy some attention. I think he must be lonely, because he poured on the guilt after I fed him." I rolled my eyes heavenward at my next admission. "I was putty in his paws after that."

Grant studied me while I spoke, and damn if I didn't fall right into the lure of his deep blue eyes. Somehow, he managed to look even better now that he had some color on his skin. The sun-kissed bronze tone set off his blond hair and the mischievous smirk that always made my panties damp.

"So, what did you need to talk about?" I asked.

"I got a phone call from Bas."

His face remained utterly impassive when he delivered the news, and I guessed he must have practiced saying the sentence a few times to do so without emotion. I couldn't miss the way his jaw pulsed at the joint, though, as he clenched it shut, or the way both fists were balled in the bedspread, either.

"Don't look so giddy about it there, chief," I teased, trying to thin some of the heavy air that settled over the room like a June morning fog. If just mentioning the almighty Shark's name was having this sort of effect on him, I was dreading the rest of the conversation before we even had it.

"I didn't actually speak to him. He left a voice mail." Grant closed his laptop and stood, captivating me as he always did with the graceful way he moved. "We must have been out of range when he called," he finally said, refocusing my attention.

The grin that took over my face was a wicked one. I knew it as sure as I knew the sun would set in the west. But I also knew I did nothing to stop it from spreading once it started. The bite in my tone matched accordingly. "Well, I'm sure that pissed him off. He called to say jump, and you weren't immediately available to ask how high."

"That's not how our relation—"

"Really?" I cut him off. "Come on, big guy. Do you really not see how that man runs you around town to do his bidding?"

"You have no idea what you're talking about, and it would

save you a lot of embarrassment to not shoot your mouth off for once," Grant fired back.

I just stared at him. I went to answer . . . and then shut my mouth again. No. Fuck that! If he wanted to throw down with me over Sebastian Shark, then the gloves would come off.

"Pardon me?" I gave my head a little shake as if clearing a mental cloud. "What did you just say to me?"

"I don't think you really need me to repeat myself, right? Especially because I'm not looking to argue with you, Rio."

"Well, I think you might be when you tell me to 'shut my mouth for once in my life.'" I gestured wildly with air quotes around the rude words he'd just let fly.

"That's not what I said."

"Grant. I heard you. I'm standing right here. I mean, I get that everyone treats me like I'm invisible, but I'm literally in the same room with you. I also have excellent hearing."

"Yes. I know where you were standing. It's rare a moment that passes when I'm not aware of your exact location, Blaze."

"Then why do you deny what you said?" I fired back.

"Because you are mistaken. I said—"

"Cut the bullshit, Twombley. Own up to your words. Just like the other day in there." I stabbed my index finger toward our cabin's bathroom. Yeah, it was high time we dealt with the big masturbating elephant in the room, too. "I heard you, by the way." I raised one eyebrow expectantly in his direction. "Do you want to explain that bullshit?"

"Bullshit?" he repeated as he prowled closer to where I stood. I wouldn't let him intimidate me though and refused to move as he neared.

"You think that was bullshit?" The dangerous look in his cobalt eyes matched the marked drop of his volume. "News flash, baby. For most people, feelings and emotions aren't considered bullshit."

He was toe-to-toe with me by now, and I had to tilt my head back to meet his threatening stare. I told myself the hasty steps I retreated were to ease the angle of my posture, but my thundering heart told a different story. When my back met the bulkhead, I knew I was truly trapped. Pinned by him—emotionally as well as physically.

After quickly closing the space I had just created between us, Grant flattened his palms on the wall on either side of my head.

"Look at me," he issued, but I couldn't—I wouldn't—comply. But that didn't matter. The bastard simply slipped his thumbs under my jaw and maneuvered my head upward. His glare was waiting—and intense.

We stayed like that, locking eyes for long, excruciating moments, before he began tracing paths back and forth along my jaw. I couldn't begin to fathom why, though the action seemed to be somehow soothing him. As if he were using my skin, and all the delicious ways he could control its reactions, to calm his temper.

"Grant—"

"No," he seethed. "You're going to hear me out. Whether you like what I have to say or not. You need to know this. That all of this—you, me, us, this isn't some fucking game for me. None of this is. I don't know when you're going to realize that, girl."

"Grant—"

"I'm not done. I'm far from done, damn it. My fucking heart is on the chopping block here, and you're the one holding the cleaver. High above your head like some fire-starting Lizzie Borden."

A profound silence, so deafening it made my ears ring, fell over our small space. We stared hard at each other, reeling in the aftermath of the seismic shift that had just occurred—that he had dealt to the tectonic plates of our relationship.

I was too stunned to move. To speak. I knew Grant was too, but I was past caring. He kept his gaze fixed on me, careful and remorseful and replete with worry. Or maybe something beyond that—but the part about me not caring was still there.

No. That wasn't true. If I didn't care, this wouldn't hurt so much. The man had just issued a critical hit to my trust, our friendship—and fuck it—my heart.

"That was beyond low, Grant Twombley," I barely whispered. Just behind my eyes, I could feel the awful sting of impending tears. In my throat, a lump was forming so fast and so large, it nearly gagged me.

"Blaze—"

It was just a gasp, but it told me a lot. The bastard seemed to realize he had royally fucked up, and for his sake, I prayed he grasped another recognition. The one about it being high time for him to shut the fuck up.

A garbled choke escaped him, and he took a tentative step back, finally releasing me. I couldn't get far enough away from him in the confines of our shared space. He went to speak, but I stopped him with a stiff, straight arm.

"Rio, please. I'm so sorry." The unmistakable sheen of tears glistened in his eyes, matching the ones now rolling down my cheeks in hot, burning streaks.

With a shake of my head, I warned him from coming any closer. I didn't want to be a fragile girl. I didn't want to be vulnerable or needy. I definitely didn't want to feel like with one more thoughtless remark, intentional or not, I would be reeling in a way so pitiful, I would physically falter.

Yet here I was. Being that girl. Doing exactly that.

I bolted from the room and gave the door a resounding slam on my way out. I jogged down the hall and considered ducking back into Robert's cabin but knew that would be the first place Grant would look. So, instead, I continued out onto the deck and made my way forward to the sunbed on the bow.

With my knees tucked beneath my cheek, I looked off to the western horizon. Each evening we chased the sun as it dipped down into the waves where Poseidon read the giant ball of fire a bedtime story. Tonight, thanks to the lingering mist of my tears, it was a smudgy but pretty blur.

But I forced myself to push past the emotions, struggling not to overanalyze everything Grant and I had just flung at each other inside. Doing so would bring more pain and sadness, and for what?

What the hell had just happened? A misunderstanding? Or was there more to it? Did Grant feel like I was finally stable enough to let the truth fly free? If so, how long had all that been festering inside him? And now that it was out, was he sincerely remorseful about it, or was he babbling those regrets just to keep me calm?

I hated having to second-guess people, and that was never something I had to do with this man: the person I thought of as my friend. I'd grown to care for and trust Grant with so many details about my life. Even the ugly, scary ones that no one else knew.

The sun sank the final inch into the water, and the last white cloud that rose up from the surface looked like a puff of smoke from an extinguished flame. I chuckled aloud at the crazy pictures my brain conjured. Time and time again, my mind's most vivid imagery involved an active fire or the destruction of prized possessions by licking flames.

I could turn it all off whenever I wanted to. Lately, the problem was, I barely wanted to. I needed the fantasies. I liked the fires. Even I didn't need a therapist to analyze the facts for me. My life was punctuated by blazes of all shapes and sizes.

I had a problem.

My hobby was getting out of hand. And this wasn't the type of problem that would be resolved quickly.

The evening sky looked desolate now. Was it my mood, or had the red-and-pink glow indeed been replaced with a lackluster gray? And what did it mean? Growing up in Maryland with the Chesapeake Bay and its tributaries so close by, the water was a part of most kids' upbringing, including mine. I scanned my childhood memory for the old saying I used to hear the adults recite.

Red at night, sailors delight. Red in the morning, sailors take warning.

"Looks like we might get a storm. Got room for one more?"

Grant's deep voice pulled me from my thoughts. The start of a grin spread across my lips before I remembered I was really pissed at him. But how silly to force feelings that weren't my natural response to him. The smile I quickly hid and the butterflies in my stomach were the real deal. I was ready for a cold beer and his warm, strong embrace.

But first I'd make him work for it—at least a little bit.

"That depends," I said coolly.

"On?"

"If you brought your knee pads," I supplied, smirking.

"Knee pads?" He tilted his head to the side, resembling

enough of an inquisitive puppy to make my pulse trip on itself.

"I'm sure you'd agree that you have some serious groveling to do, Tree. And everyone knows the best groveling is done from your—"

Before I could finish my sentence, six and a half feet of solid man thudded to the boat deck in front of me. His left eye seemed to twitch involuntarily with the shock of pain from his stunt, but it didn't distract from the impulsive gallantry of the gesture. If anything, my runaway pulse was now off to a full, flummoxed gallop.

I scooted to the edge of the sunbed to inspect for damage to Grant's patellae and the boat's fiberglass. While he knelt motionlessly, I raked my gaze up his body and came to rest on his hopeful eyes.

"You may begin," I issued with a dismissive but teasing wave.

Grant inched his way closer to me and placed his palms on my knees. When I didn't protest the physical contact, he spread my legs apart and settled between them, making our position intimate.

"Don't get any big ideas. You're supposed to be groveling, remember?"

"Baby," he breathed more than spoke. "I'm so sorry." As the proud man bowed his head with regret, he continued, "I was a total jackass before, and you have every right to be pissed off."

"Well, thanks for your permission. I feel so much better."

He huffed. "You didn't let me finish."

Despite my staunchest efforts, I could feel the corners of my lips quirking. "You don't have much experience with this whole groveling thing, do you? I can tell you're way out of your element."

He cracked a small smirk too. "You're right, Blaze. I'm not usually the one on my knees."

I rolled my eyes and pushed his shoulder so hard he toppled off-balance and fell back to sit on his heels. He popped right back up, employing that athletic grace that always turned my belly into a gymnastics meet, before wrapping his large hand around the back of my neck so quickly, I didn't have time to process what was happening. When he pulled me so close that our foreheads were touching, I could feel his panting breaths fan across my face.

"You're testing me, woman. I'm trying here. Cut me some slack."

My breathing was just as ragged, but I managed to answer. "I'm not sure you deserve it, Tree. Are you?"

"No. I probably don't." He stunned me again, this time with his fervent sincerity. "But do you hear me saying I'm sorry? I fucked up. I was pissed off, and I made some terribly insensitive remarks. It doesn't make it right, it doesn't give me an excuse, but I am apologizing."

More of his unvarnished honesty mixed with the most earnest I'd ever seen him led to my ultimate undoing. Once more, tears built before they came—and now, there was no way to choke them back. I hated crying, especially in front of other people. The last thing I needed with this man was another open show of vulnerability.

"Oh, baby." Grant's tender croon was like salt in an open wound. "Don't cry."

He completely ignored my attempts to hold him at bay and hugged me tightly to his chest, wrapping his long arms around my back. God, he felt so good. So strong. So safe. So perfect and terrifying all at the same time.

Somewhere deep inside me, a dam burst, and I began to sob. Precisely what I was trying to avoid. But Grant held me while I trembled and rocked with it. Even by the end, when I sniffled and sputtered from it.

"Better?" he finally cooed, leaning back a bit to see my face. He stroked my short hair back off my forehead, and his long fingers felt divine scraping across my scalp. I wanted to curse and shout all over again at the unfairness of the universe bringing this fantastic man directly in my path at the most fucked-up time of my existence.

"Blaze?" he asked quietly, and the sincerity of his tone captured my full attention.

"Hmm?" The sound had to be a stand-in for an answer because I didn't trust my voice with recognizable words yet. I observed him through the gaze I narrowed again, concerned about what he was about to ask. After all, it hadn't been the first time he'd seen me fall apart, and maybe he was over it. This time, for good.

"Can I get up yet?"

It was the ideal break to the heavy emotional cloud that had settled over us. We burst out laughing as Grant unfolded his tall frame and groaned. As he stood, he massaged his leg muscles, and I watched with hungry interest.

"Totally worth it." He gave me a quick wink. The mischief that twinkled in his midnight eyes could've been one of the stars that were currently trying to make its presence seen in the overhead sky.

Once again, I was touched by the many facets of this complex man. For every panty-slaying move he knew how to execute, there was a genuine, kind, well-mannered gesture to balance it out.

Simply put, Grant Twombley was perfect.

"Do you have any flaws, Tree? At all?" I stood on the cushion of the sunbed with my bare feet, bringing Grant about eye level with my breasts. After a fast hum of approval, he quickly gripped my hips, and I held his shoulders while finishing my thought. "It's so unfair to the rest of mankind that you are this perfect."

He looked up to meet my gaze. "You think I'm perfect?"

"Well..." I tilted my head, barely able to hide my playful smile. "I think some women would think you are."

"I don't care what other women think," he countered. "What's on your mind, Blaze?"

He issued it with such intense interest, I was almost taken aback. He really cared about my answer, and it showed in his steady gaze, his complete focus. I owed him the same with my answer, which I gave after a moment of quiet thoughtfulness.

"This trip definitely has given me a lot of time to think," I confessed. "But I'm pretty sure it was your devious plan all the while," I accused with absolutely no anger.

"Well, that and a lot of uninterrupted sex."

"Oh, yeah. There is that." I grinned and knocked his shoulder.

"Quit trying to change the subject," he chided before pulling my face toward his and planting a quick kiss on the tip of my nose. "Come on. Let me get settled in here. I really want to hear what you have to say."

He climbed onto the bed and then settled against the cushioned backrest of the inset bed. Once there, he motioned for me to come to him. While his embrace was so tempting, I hesitated for a few seconds. It was already difficult for me to discuss self-discovery topics. Throw in an audience of one very attentive, charming, good-looking, tall, imposing, Dominant man and, well, yeah... My nerves skyrocketed to Venus and back.

But damn it, I had to start somewhere. And Grant's larger frame always provided a safe harbor for me, on top of his uncanny instinct about knowing when I craved the feeling of his protection. I needed that right now, more than ever before. His physical presence lent me the strength to deal with the topic that had left me emotionally and psychologically crippled for most of my life.

We lay that way for a few minutes. Each time I thought I was ready to start talking, I'd chicken out. Grant knew I was having a hard time kicking off the conversation, when he finally said, "Take all the time you need, baby. It's just us here, and we have nowhere else to be."

I inhaled his cologne one more time and enjoyed how the ocean mist brought out the familiar citrus and cedar notes. That, combined with his reassuring hold, at last imbued me with the courage to talk. "Thank you for being patient. I thought I knew exactly what I wanted to say, but I keep stumbling over it all in my mind."

He dipped his head down, bussing the top of my head. "Like I said, baby, no rush."

I traced some designs into the center of his chest while taking another deep breath. "Well, first... I know I haven't been easy to deal with lately, and I'm sorry about that."

"Rio. You have good reason to be on edge." He started rhythmic strokes up and down my back, soothing me beyond measure. Would there ever be a moment when the man didn't know exactly what my body, mind, and soul needed? God, I hoped not. But this was about more than my stress levels right now. This was about me confronting the ways they'd made me act out.

"You can't keep making excuses for me," I asserted. "At some point, I have to take responsibility for myself and my actions."

"I like taking care of you. I wish you would understand that. It feeds my Dominant nature."

"I do understand that. But taking care of a few everyday needs for me is one thing. Enabling me to live in denial about a mental health problem is another thing altogether." I watched him with a fixed stare until he answered. After he gave a gentle nod, I was more comfortable moving into the more practiced part of what I'd wanted to say. I didn't want to give him a lecture, and I certainly wasn't interested in blaming him for anything. For the first time in my life, I had some clarity on the way I was feeling and what was going on with me. It was essential to share it all with him if he was going to continue to be in my life.

"Sometimes when you care about someone, the hardest thing you ever have to do is sit off to the side and watch them hurt—or even worse, to hurt themselves."

He pushed out a meaningful breath. "Yeah. I understand that."

"I know." As I said it, he took my hand in his. I paused to smile. Such a small action, but the silent display of his support meant so much. Once again, I was infused with new courage to go on.

"But as we both know, a person has to be ready to see a problem for herself." I smiled coyly in his direction while using that particular pronoun. "And until she's at that place, she may be blind to what everyone can see. But then, one day, something clicks into place, and she moves into the light. The place where she realizes she needs help. But more than that ... that she really wants it."

I stared back at him over my shoulder for a couple beats, hoping like hell he was hearing what I was trying to say. I got my answer in the most perfect way, as he lifted our joined hands to his lips and kissed our knuckles where they came together.

"Whatever you need from me, baby, I'm here for you. You're the strongest woman I've ever met by far. If anyone can rise to a challenge and conquer it, it's you. I also know you're not a quitter. So even if there is tough work ahead? You'll do that too. I believe in you, Blaze."

My voice faltered when I tried to speak, and I could actually feel my chin tremble. "Th-Thank you," I finally managed to whimper. I turned fully and climbed onto him like a little bear cub. I just needed to be enveloped in the haven of this man's arms. I was scared to death of what was wrong with me, and feeling Grant all around me would give me the comfort and strength I craved.

While I cried into the crook of his neck, Grant quietly rocked me in his lap. When I finally exhausted the very last tear and sniffle I could possibly produce, he leaned back to get a better look at me. After surveying the damage, he grinned that charming but devilish grin I had come to enjoy so much.

"Uh-oh." I narrowed my watery gaze, waiting to see what had the man smirking.

"What, uh-oh?" he asked, affronted that I seemed suspicious. He did, however, produce a handkerchief from a pocket somewhere and handed me the convenient white linen cloth.

"Nice try, Twombley. Don't forget, I know you as well as you know me, and that grin"—I stabbed my index finger toward his smug smile—"usually means trouble." I sat forward on his lap but only moved about six inches before he stopped me and hauled me back against his chest.

Grant pressed a wet, lingering kiss just below my ear, and I shivered when the cool night air met the dampness on my skin. "Where do you think you're going?" he growled against my flesh.

"I just figured you'd want to get up."

"Oh, baby," he groaned. "Can't you feel it?" He ground his cock up into my ass as if answering his own question. "The only thing I'm interested in getting up?" He thrust his hips up into my bottom again before finishing his comment. "Already is. The question now is . . . what shall we do about it?"

CHAPTER NINE

GRANT

Three days later, we were strolling through the palm-lined streets of Honolulu for the last time. Our port of call would soon be in our wake, and we'd be cruising home toward Los Angeles. Many boxes had been checked off the mental list of things I wanted to accomplish on this getaway, but a few essential items remained.

Each time I thought I finally had an opportunity to address one of the issues left unspoken, we were either interrupted by the crew, fell into bed in a tangle of lips, tongues, and naked body parts, or simply fell into bed from exhaustion. After Rio's night of self-discovery on the bow of the boat, I started to suspect the brat was doing it on purpose just so she wouldn't have to deal with more hard topics.

The woman blew my mind that night—even though I always knew she possessed the bravery to face her fears. Shit . . . most of the time, it felt like I believed in her more than she believed in herself. However, the stars aligned just right for her self-empowerment that night or some sort of cosmic dribble like that. The end result was what was worth celebrating. The cherry on top of the personal growth sundae? Rio came to all the conclusions on her own. Nothing was forced by me or anyone else.

Hearing her finally admit she needed professional help lightened my mood more than I thought possible. By the next morning, I was even ready to call Bas and Abbi and apologize for being such an irritable ass lately—until Rio saw the number I was dialing and snatched my phone from my hand and refused to give it back. Little did she know, sticking my device down her tiny sleep shorts didn't provide much of a deterrent. More like a challenge I was ready and willing to accept.

And conquer with a victory flag flying at a very stiff full mast. Silly girl.

"What are you Mr. Smiles about?" Rio asked, bumping her shoulder into my side as we walked. I used the moment as an excuse to sling my arm around her shoulder and keep her body close as we ducked under the awning of a little jewelry shop.

"Just thinking about some of my favorite memories from this trip." I made sure to capture her gaze before finishing. "I'm happy we got to spend this time together and away from LA."

She tentatively rested her palm on my chest and smiled. "I am too. Thank you for risking so much to do this."

It was such a tender moment for her. For us. None of her usual smart mouth comebacks or bitter comments to cover her discomfort with dealing with emotions. The public display of affection, however small it was, was an unexpected surprise too.

"I'd do it all again. In a heartbeat," I said, my voice quieter now that we were inside the shop and away from the bustle of the touristy street. "So, what are you looking for in here?"

She turned a pair of earrings between her fingers a few times before setting them down and answering. "I wanted to bring something back for Hannah. Why don't you find something for Reina?"

With a scrunched face, I decisively shook my head. "I'm not sure giving my executive assistant jewelry strikes the right tone."

"I'm not suggesting a diamond ring, Grant. What's wrong with a nice pair of earrings? Look how pretty these are." She thrust a random pair in my direction, and I took them like an obedient shopping companion.

I barely glanced at the dangling disasters before setting them back on the counter. "I think I'll stick to the nice-sized holiday bonus I give her every year. It works for us, so why upset the apple cart?"

Rio shrugged and carried two items toward the register, where a smiling local woman waited to help her. "Suit yourself. Let me just pay for these, and I'll be ready."

"Take your time. How does lunch sound?" I called out to her while I riffled through a rack of bathing suits. A little black two-piece caught my eye, and I wondered how much of a fuss the woman would kick up if I bought it for her.

Little crocheted triangles made up the skimpy top, and there wasn't much more to the bottoms. Another saleswoman appeared by my side while Rio continued her animated conversation with the woman behind the register.

"That one looks great on." She smiled warmly and then nodded toward Rio at the other end of the shop. "For her?"

"Maybe. I'm not sure if she would let me buy it for her, though. She can be . . . stubborn," I finally filled in.

"I'll get a bag, and you can just round off the price if you're paying cash." She leaned even closer so we could conspire about the purchase. "That way, you can surprise her when the time is right?" she suggested, hoping to close a sale.

I had to hand it to her—she knew the art of the deal.

"Yeah, all right." I quickly pulled out my wallet and handed the woman some cash, and she darted off for a bag. We finished our mission well before Rio wrapped up her conversation and made her way back to me.

"Ready?" she asked cheerfully, and we moved out onto the sidewalk. "I wasn't hungry until you mentioned food. Now I'm starving." While standing on the balls of her feet, she gripped my forearm for balance and tried to see over the throng of people. "I think there was a fish taco place a couple shops down that way." Rio sank back down to her flat feet but looked up at me over the tops of her sunglasses. "Isn't that the direction of the marina?" she asked with a bit of confusion.

"I think this place really agrees with you. You're positively radiant right now." Before she could protest, because fuck, I knew she would, I bent and wrapped my arms around her waist and hauled her body flush against mine, lifting her off the ground.

"Looking lost like an obvious tourist?" she asked while stifling a giggle. People grumbled as they had to divert their course to walk around us, but I didn't care. While I had her body pressed against mine, I couldn't think of much else.

I kissed the tip of her sun-kissed nose and then her glossy lips before letting her slide down the front of my body until her feet touched the ground again. The sticky strawberry goo she had on her lips was on mine then too, and I tasted it with a grimace.

"Oh my God, I wish I had my camera out for that. That was priceless." Mischief transformed her entire face, and I was the one wishing I had a camera at the ready. This woman captivated me in so many different ways, I felt like a love-sick teenager again.

Except, when I was a teenager, I never had time for feelings like these. I was busy watching my back on the streets and worrying about staying one step ahead of law enforcement when Bas and I were up to trouble—which, let's face it, was all the damn time.

"How can you stand that on your lips all day?" I asked, digging into my pocket and hoping I remembered a handkerchief, even though I had on casual shorts.

"It's the small price a girl pays to have lips all the boys want to kiss," she answered.

The mere thought of any other "boy" kissing what was mine had a menacing sound clawing up my throat before I could intercept it.

"Easy, killer," she said, patting the center of my chest.

Quickly grabbing her delicate hand, I held it over my thundering heart. "I don't think I could be responsible for my actions if I had to witness you kissing another man."

Though she held my gaze for a beat or two, I couldn't read her expression through her sunglasses. Talking about having an exclusive relationship would likely send her running for the hills, and . . . Well, shit. What did I know about the subject myself?

So when she blurted out one of her random topic shifts, I actually felt a sigh of relief escape my lungs. "I think maybe I'll indulge in a beer today. What do you think? Doesn't that sound good?" Rio asked, rather than address my premature possessiveness.

Still, I couldn't help but chuckle as we started walking again. Even though I was grateful for the topic change, it had to have been the clumsiest I'd ever witnessed, even from her. And she was giving her go-to tactic a hearty workout this trip.

Anytime the subject shifted to one she didn't want to discuss, whether it was because she was uncomfortable or didn't want to face particular emotions, she would hurl us headlong into another conversation without a warm-up or introduction. The routine topic whiplash I sustained had really sharpened my communication skills during the trip, though. If I still had a job when we got back to California, the new talent would serve me well in the boardroom.

"Two for lunch, please," Rio said with a shiny-lipped smile when we approached the eatery's hostess podium.

"Inside or out on the patio?" the server asked my girl—until she caught sight of me and began something close to a visual molestation.

While I worked on my charmingly chill skills, Rio was clearly growing impatient with the woman's blatant perusal. One glance at her terse profile, even from my vantage point, had me bending over to cut off the woman's fire while it was still manageable embers.

"Please tell her where you want to sit so we can move out of the doorway, baby," I rumbled directly into her ear. The whole time, I kept a hand splayed possessively across her hip, and I greedily took advantage of the chance to get in a nip to the sensitive skin of her neck.

I knew every single reaction of Rio's body by that point. They were cataloged in my memory like short clips I could call up and play on command. As soon as her breathing hitched from my sensual little bite, I knew what would come next. When I stood to my full height again, a deep flush of arousal would paint her flesh from the gentle swell of her breasts up to where my teeth had just been. I couldn't fucking wait to watch.

"I'm sorry." Rio leaned closer to the girl to get an obvious look at her name tag. "Candace, is it?" She worked in a sweet smile before continuing, "Do you work out on the patio as well as inside the dining room?"

The young woman looked a bit confused but replied, "Uh, no. I stay here by the door when I'm not showing people to their tables."

"Good, good." Rio nodded with effervescence. "We'll take the patio, then."

"Uhh, okay. Follow me, please?" The poor girl was so confused and could definitely tell something she didn't like had just happened but couldn't quite work out the details. I wasn't much help for easing her nerves, already indulging the happiness that swelled through me from my Blaze's possessive display. After the wonderful way she'd let me touch her back at the boutique, I was feeling like the goddamned king of the free world.

We hadn't publicly shown affection to one another before today, and damn, it felt good. I never considered how much I'd been missing that, or how much I'd enjoy it, but I felt like I could fuck this girl on the table, and it still wouldn't be enough of a public claim. I'd known months ago I felt this way about Rio, but judging by the look of confusion taking over my little pixie's features, she was having trouble working out her own similar feelings.

Once we were seated and had ordered a couple of beers, I leaned back in the chair and stretched my legs beneath the table. The new position gave me a long minute to just study the captivating woman sitting across from me. It was another perfect moment for my mental video library. Perhaps its portrait gallery too. Rio looked over the menu as if she were going to be quizzed on its contents afterward. Her usually pale skin was lightly tanned, and her facial features were relaxed. The only thing that gave away the storm inside her mind was how her eyes bounced and darted from picture to explanation and then on to the next item. Her pupils scanned so rapidly; it was fascinating that she could be processing any of it.

"What are you getting?" she finally asked, looking up from the lengthy menu. Confusion twisted her adorable features, and I chuckled before answering.

"I thought you were jonesing for fish tacos?" I reminded instead of actually answering the question she asked.

"But they have so many delicious-looking things. Now I can't decide."

"I had a feeling this was going to happen the minute I saw the size of the menu."

"Sean always says the—"

Well, shit.

After cutting herself off midsentence, she was prisoner to a wide, terrified stare. First, she just looked at me with those incredibly expressive eyes, as if I held the balm that would relieve the pain she'd just rekindled. Then my girl darted her gaze to every corner of the room, as if expecting her late husband's ghost to arrive at one of the entrances and ask to be seated at our table. A pained sound escaped, even though she tried to press her lips together in a seam.

"Okay, Blaze. Breathe." I said the words as conversationally as possible so the patrons sitting closest to us wouldn't notice anything out of the ordinary. The dining room was crowded and loud and, I suspected, over the fire marshal's maximum occupancy limit by at least twenty people. Tables were unusually close to one another, so our neighbors were within earshot.

When she didn't transition from her steady blank stare, I asked, "Hey? Want to get some air? We can order to go or just eat on the boat instead?"

Her hands were in their usual place in her lap. Likely she had been digging her nails into her thighs beneath the table to focus her rioting nerves. Often, she grew anxious in public settings like this and used the trick to stay calm. Unfortunately, I couldn't subtly squeeze them in mine to snap her focus back to the present, so I waited while a few more beats passed. When she still hadn't snapped out of the trance she had slipped into, I did the unthinkable. I was going to get in serious hot water, but I couldn't see another option. Under the table, I drew back at the knee and kicked her shin.

"Asshole!" Rio yelled. The only eight people remaining who hadn't noticed her up to that point sure as hell did then.

Yeah, that was shitty. But at least it worked. "Welcome back," I muttered, trying not to attract more attention.

"Fuck, Grant. Seriously?"

"Sorry, baby."

"Sorry? Really? That's all you've got after a stunt like that? I'm sure it's already turning black and blue." She leaned down, nearly resting her cheek on the tablecloth to rub her abused shin.

I leaned across the table and growled, "What did you want me to do? You were staring like a zombie. Half the staff was already panicking like they'd have to perform some first-aid procedure from a class they didn't pay attention in."

Rio extinguished the fiery glare with which she'd nearly been roasting me alive. "Sorry," she muttered instead, blowing out an onerous exhale. "We can just go. I'm not really hungry now anyway." Her sorrowful caramel stare never left her twisting fingers until I reached across the table and wrapped my palm over her knuckles.

"Blaze."

"What?" she snapped.

"Look at me."

Christ. One step forward, two steps back. Would life forever be like this with the woman?

Easy answer on that one. If it was, then she was worth it.

She was worth everything.

Slowly, she leveled her chin with the table again and met my waiting stare.

"You did not embarrass me. There isn't a single thing you could do that would embarrass me. Do you understand that?" I asked in the most serious tone I could muster.

"You say that now."

"Well, it's true." I paused thoughtfully, cocking my head. "Oh, hold up. I haven't seen you dance yet. Is it that bad?"

"Be careful now, Tree—" She chuckled at first, but the sound gave way to a real laugh. I was instantly grateful that I had quickly decided to inject a little humor into my last comment to lighten the mood.

"But seriously for a second." She was the one to put her hand on mine now, and I wasn't going to be a dumb shit and waste the opportunity. I spread my fingers and let her slim feminine ones fall between them, locking us together in a small way. My heart swelled a bit more when, instead of the usual tugging away, Rio squeezed her hand tighter with mine and finished her thought.

"Before our server comes back, did you want to leave? I don't want you to be uncomfortable now," my beautiful woman said.

"Well, I'm still hungry and we're already seated," I commented while scanning the crowded restaurant. "But I want you to enjoy yourself, too, so I will do whatever you want. You make the call." I really hoped she would choose to stay because, at some point, she was going to have to stop running and face Sean's death head-on.

Maybe I wasn't the right person to help her through that particular struggle in her life. Obviously I'd lost all objectivity on the subject of her personal, private life. But when it came to her happiness, I cared as much as—no, more than—everyone else, that she saw her way through this grieving and healing and found joy in living again.

Our waitress approached, and I looked to Rio with a hopeful nod. She both surprised me and made me so proud that instead of asking for the check for our drinks, she placed her lunch order. I followed suit, and when the server walked off, I scooped up her hands in mine. It was becoming harder and harder to not be touching her all the time. Even if just in some small way.

Of course, the bigger ways were so much more fun...

"I had an idea today. I wanted to get your thoughts on it. Also, I have something I need to ask you..." Rio looked to me nervously while she sprinkled salt on the communal basket of chips the waitress placed between us.

"Yes, we should definitely get a sex swing for the Naples house." I pretended to be preoccupied with something on my phone, just to mess with her by throwing the random comment out nonchalantly. When she didn't respond after a couple beats, I looked up to find her frozen with a chip halfway to her mouth. A wide grin was plastered across her face.

"Oh, I see my queen likes that idea, too. Noted." I'm sure

my grin matched hers then.

"You're damn crazy, do you know that?"

I winked at her over the rim of my beer, partly because I knew it infuriated her, mostly because I already had the glass to my lips when asked the question, and the heat we had been shopping in really made me thirsty.

"What I really wanted to talk to you about . . ." She shifted uncomfortably in her chair, and her gaze moved around the dining room again, much slower this time, not the wild, unfocused way they had before. When it seemed as though she was going to take a second lap visually, I spoke up.

"Baby, do you remember one of the first times we met for lunch after I stopped working with you at Abstract? We met at the Bunker Hill Steps?"

"Yep. Sure do." She smiled at the memory, too. "Empanadas, if I recall."

"That's right," I agreed while my beam grew in direct proportion to hers. "You told me you wished more people would just say what they meant, would stop beating around the bush. Do it, girl. Speak your mind. It's me." I thumped the middle of my chest. "I may actually be one of the least judgmental people in LA." I finished the last of my beer and waited for her to speak.

"Tall, handsome, and a lock stock memory, too." The little imp narrowed her eyes playfully. "You're quite the package, Mr. Twombley."

"I listen. Because . . . you matter to me. But if you don't understand that by now, you're never going to." I leaned over more, to really grab her attention. "And I'd be happy to reacquaint you with my package, Ms. Gibson."

The red flush—the one I was completely addicted to

coaxing from her—spread across her chest and moved up her neck. If we weren't in the middle of a crowded patio in the heart of Honolulu, one more illicit comment or perfectly placed kiss or bite, and she'd go slack in my arms. My cock swelled painfully in my shorts at the thought, but fortunately she'd gotten back to girding herself for the confession at hand. Or whatever it was. After tossing back the rest of her beer like a frat boy, she sat up straighter and directly met my gaze.

"Okay, here goes." She searched my face for a long moment, and I silently gave her all the strength I could. Not that she actually needed it. She was one of the strongest people I knew. I just wished she'd believe that too. "I—well, I went ahead and joined an online support group."

She took a deep breath and held it. She frantically studied my face for a reaction.

"Hey. Breathe, baby, so you don't hyperventilate. Please."

She shook her head as if my request had been in ancient Greek. "Breathe?" she sputtered. "That's seriously all you have for me here?"

"Of course not."

But she wasn't any calmer as I stood abruptly and moved into the empty chair to my right, repositioning myself right next to her. No way could I accept this news from her with nothing but a polite smile and a few pats on her hands. This was huge. Important. A gigantic, courageous step forward. I had to show her that, with all my actions as well as my words. She had to feel every ounce of my sincerity, pride, and admiration. Nothing else would be sufficient. I was committed to the cause despite her bewildered gasp as I firmly wrapped her hands in mine.

"Grant? Wh-What are you—"

The wooden legs of her chair protested when I gripped her seat and dragged her to face me. With my knees, I formed brackets on either side of hers. I hoped like hell I wasn't scaring her with my exuberance, but shit... I couldn't help it. This was the first move toward self-help she had ever made. While it was a small step, it really was a fucking step, and I wanted to acknowledge the achievement. Most of all, I yearned to celebrate her.

"I'm so damn proud of you," I affirmed, delving my gaze as deep into hers as I could. Her wide, inquisitive irises were kissed with flecks of gold thanks to the Hawaiian sun, and I added it to the mental list of things I would miss when we left here.

"Do you want to tell me more about it?"

Of course, our server arrived at that exact moment with our meals, and while I wanted to continue our little two-person commemoration, her attention fractured the moment the food arrived. I couldn't help but share the distraction. We were both hungry after being on the town all morning, so I swiveled my chair back toward the table, and we wasted no time tucking into the plates set in front of us.

While we enjoyed our lunch, I let Rio set the conversational pace. She explained what led her to join the support group of other young Southern California widows. I was hoping, in small part, the support group she'd found was for pyromania and similar addictions, but Rome wasn't built in a day, and I was grateful for this much. It was also quite possible that the issues surrounding her hobby needed to be handled with a therapist in a one-on-one setting.

This group was an outstanding move forward. I was more positive about that as she started filling in the details. Since the group was online, she could choose to attend meetings every day or as infrequently as once a month. They also met in person on occasion, but she wasn't ready to commit to that sort of interaction yet. Or at least that's how she explained it.

"I'm proud of you, Rio," I repeated and meant it twice as much as before. "If there's anything I can do to help, please let me know. I know I don't have the experience you've had." I shook my head. "The only 'significant person' I've lost by societal standards was more an anchor on me than a set of wings. But I want to see you live fully and healthily again."

"Thank you, Grant." The amber flecks in her eyes were clear and joyous. She released a breath like a hundred pounds left her at the same time. "You've been such an amazing friend through all of this. I mean it. I don't deserve you in my corner."

"Bullshit," I flung, until she leaned closer to peck my cheek. That part was bullshit too, because now I absolutely needed to feel her lips on mine. I told her so by palming her cheek and tugging her over once more. Her lips beneath mine… Holy shit, the island gods really were smiling on me today. Her mouth was warm and sweet and welcoming, meaning it was damn near impossible to keep the gesture chaste in the middle of the restaurant patio, but ideas began to flood me for what we could do back on the boat.

By the time we returned to the yacht, we had full bellies, tired eyes, and sore feet. Neither one of us was used to walking very far in our workday, though Rio did spend much of hers on her feet. But my heart was lighter than it had been in weeks. I finally had hope again for a future that included a healthy existence for the woman I cared so deeply about—with emotions that were burgeoning more and more with every passing day. And while the magic of the Pacific and the spell of aloha certainly hadn't been deterrents, I was damn sure my mind and heart would be right here, exactly in this space, if we were still in the normal bustle and burn of Los Angeles.

That was why I dared to keep feeling this way. To keep stoking the vision of a forever inspired by my beautiful Blaze. To keep holding out hope for what all this meant for her and me—together.

Because when she was ready—if she were ever ready—I'd be right here, waiting for her.

I wanted a shot at happiness with Rio Gibson. No. I demanded it. And I wasn't going to give up until fate forked it over.

CHAPTER TEN

RIO

"And Abbigail? She's doing okay?"

I strained to hear the side of the conversation I was privy to. Well, sort of privy to, seeing how I was currently eavesdropping on this part as well. Grant left me in the hot tub on the yacht's lower aft deck with a promise to return quickly. That was before Sebastian announced his son had finally made his entrance into the world a few hours earlier in the day. But since he took the call, the almighty Shark had captured Grant's full attention.

Jealousy was definitely not surging through my veins. Really...how ridiculous would that be? After all, if we were getting technical, Kaisan was my nephew, not Grant's. So why wasn't I the person taking the phone call with the fabulous news?

The answer was as close, but far away, as observing my reflection in the gentle swishes of the hot tub's waters. I'd long since climbed out and turned off the tub's jets but lingered at the edge with my feet in the light-aqua water.

Who was the woman returning my rapt gaze?

Once upon a time, I was clearer about that response. About everything I wanted out of my life and the people I included in it. Sean and I were young when we met but not so giddy and silly that we didn't recognize the good thing we had. Needless to say, we didn't date long before deciding—to our parents' dismay—to get married and move to California. I couldn't remember my life without him because I'd never been an adult without him in the landscape. And yes, that vista included dreams of starting our own family. I'd lie awake night after night, thinking about having a baby of my own. About rocking my own child, sweet and perfect, in my arms. It would be a chance to get things right in my life. To find the piece of me that was inexplicably missing. Becoming a mother would complete me; I'd been so sure of it.

On most days, as much as I had once wanted it, I was thankful that Sean and I never had a child. I could eventually figure out how to pick up the pieces of my broken heart—my broken life—and get on with it all. I *would* figure all that out. I had to believe that. But if I had a child with the man, too? Had to look into a child's face that looked just like his father's, day in and day out? I don't think my already precarious mental health could endure cruelty that severe.

Now, I didn't even know the person who stared back at me from the mirror. I barely knew what food I wanted to eat or what music I enjoyed listening to. Everything I once loved was entwined with bitter memories that used to be sweet. Old dates that used to hold special meanings now just held hollow ghosts. Nothing seemed pristine anymore.

Was I acting melodramatic? Maybe. But being a widow was still a fairly new status for me. And so far, I was really sucking at it. I had no idea how to view the things in my old world with these new eyes. Because while things were theoretically the same, they were completely different, too.

Trying to explain that to the people around me was harder

than I imagined, but now that I'd joined the online support group, I was hoping to get some tips on navigating my new existence. One way or the other, though, I had to get my shit together.

I didn't even know how to enjoy myself ... myself.

Step one seemed pretty obvious, though. I had to find joy in living again. I could do it—and, with help, I would. Just not right this second. Especially not as Grant's voice gained volume when he came toward the back of the boat again. From what I could make out, he was wrapping up his phone call with a lot of good wishes for both Sebastian and Abbigail, and the stabbing ache was back. Right in the center of my chest.

Damn it.

But what was this damn feeling if not jealousy? Something close to anger was dancing right on the fringe of my temperament, but that didn't make sense. Why would I be angry with Abbigail for safely and successfully delivering her son? I truly wanted nothing but the best for my sister-in-law. While I could openly admit that previously I'd had difficulty staying positive about her pregnancy, so many of those issues were no longer active or valid. Not with Sean gone. Especially not with the time I'd been gifted to start really looking at my issues.

The remarkable gift ... possible because of my towering, golden-haired benefactor, now striding back into view on the deck. He was still on the phone, head bent low and shoulders bunched with more than a touch of tension. I didn't have any trouble hearing his dialogue now.

"Look, Bas. You know you're my best friend. My brother. I couldn't be happier for you right now, and a large part of me wishes I had been there for your son's arrival." Grant finished it by pinching the bridge of his nose, which I could only assume was in frustration. He looked up to find me cautiously watching, though I desperately tried to eke out an encouraging smile instead. Without acknowledging me, he turned and shuffled a couple feet away to the railing.

And why did that sting so much?

"No, I'm not telling you where we are, and I won't sell her out, either. I'm not admitting to something that just isn't true. No matter what damn day of the year it is." Grant shook his head, funneling that vehemence into his next words at the asshole who couldn't see him. "God, you're a fucking piece of work, you know that?" He took a calming breath and said, "Go be with your new family, Sebastian. I'll call you in a couple of days. Please give Abbigail my best. I'll have Rio call once Abbi and the baby have had a chance to rest."

With that, my handsome white knight ended the call. After pivoting to set his phone down on the deck chair where we had first set our towels, he paused again, his head hung low, chin tucked tightly to his chest. He was in the same spot for so long, I thought he might be having second thoughts about rejoining me, but he finally turned and walked back over.

"Hey."

"Hey." He got it out on another heavy breath.

"You okay?" I said gently. "We can just go back to the cabin, if you'd rather? I'll scratch your head?" Clearly, the time he'd endured on the phone had ramped his stress to a level I hadn't seen in days. No, forget stressed. He sounded exhausted.

"Nah, Blaze. Let's stay out here."

I nodded, hoping the fresh air, night sky, and easy companionship would be of some help. My heart panged as I held his hand tight while we got back into the water together. Just two hours ago, he'd been virile and exuberant, the gorgeously perfect picture of living and loving life. I had finally been feeling like returning to Los Angeles would be manageable instead of insurmountable. As with all things alongside this incredible man, it seemed like getting through daily life would be possible again. He seemed to be excited about it too—until Sebastian's call shattered our happy reverie.

"So, as you can probably guess, Kaisan arrived earlier today." Grant's announcement was quiet, accompanied by a genuine smile, after he settled into the water and allowed a bank of jets to pummel his back. "Congratulations, by the way, Auntie."

I was equally sincere about my soft laugh as he pulled my buoyant body closer until I straddled his lap in the corner of the spa. I released a blissful sigh, forgetting all about his standoffish move from a few minutes ago. It wasn't hard, once I was surrounded in the muscled magic of his embrace, the perfect strength of his nearness. I reveled in the view of his serene expression, betraying he'd fallen prey to the same effect from me. Yeah, this was addicting...and yeah, I was damn sure I didn't care. Not right now. We had come to need each other's physical touch more and more with each passing day—though I was fairly certain my dependency outweighed his. His presence was like a balm for my aching heart and soul, especially during my darkest and most dismal hours. I wasn't going to give it up until he told me I had to.

A bank of jets pummeled Grant's back from every angle where we were situated in the deepest water.

"Christ, this feels good," he preached to the nighttime sky with an extended groan. I simply stared, fantasizing about nibbling his Adam's apple, where it protruded from his extended throat.

"What's going to happen when we get back? That phone call didn't sound like running away made any of my problems disappear." When Grant brought his face level with mine, I berated myself for continuing on this topic. Knowing the deep furrows of stress that etched his beautiful face were because of me shattered my heart.

"I am so sorry," I murmured.

"Why are you apologizing?" he finally asked. Even his voice sounded weary and resigned.

"Don't you think I see what's going on here? The stress in your life, between you and your best friend? I know it's because of me." I pulled out of his arms and moved off his lap to sit beside him. The intimate position was suddenly too close. Too stifling. "I'm crazy, Grant, not dumb."

His first response was much more of a growl. When the air stilled again and I found the courage to look back to Grant, he was waiting with words. "Rio. It's not because of you. It's because of Bas." Grant slashed his palm through the froth on the surface before he continued. "It's because of his tyrannical, controlling method of going about everything in his life. You happen to be caught in the middle of the storm this time, but it could have easily been someone else."

His own growl was his interruption, as he gave in to staring out into the night. For a long moment he peered even harder, as if spotting something way off on the horizon. Finally, he shook his head slowly and went on, "What he's doing with all this is wrong, and the bastard knows it. Bas is trying to avert everyone's attention from the faulty equipment that killed your husband, even if that means dragging you through the mud by spotlighting your breakdown the night of the accident. But the asshole doesn't care what that will do to me if he does that. He certainly doesn't care what it will do to you."

"How can he think something like this would touch him? It's old news at this point, and it's such an insignificant event in his day. Not to mention, how can my crazy behavior be more interesting than the big bad Sebastian Shark's fancy building being cursed?" With a dismissive wave, I finished, "Or whatever. That seems like a juicier headline to me." But then I was the one doing the head shaking. "I really don't get why he would risk your friendship over this."

"Because it is still a juicy story," he stressed.

I grabbed a chance for my turn with the deep frown too. "I seriously don't follow."

"Come on. Picture the sound bite. 'Grieving widow's dramatic act of retribution.'" He fanned his hands through the air between us while he predicted the story's headline. While I understood the effect he was going for, the whole thing looked too damn funny not to crack another smile. Grant huffed. "This really isn't funny, Rio."

"Agreed. But honestly? Your jazz hands could use some work."

He flashed a smirk—likely the sexiest version I'd ever seen of it. "Well, I think that's the only skill you've said my hands needed improvement with."

"Hmmm." I hummed in mock contemplation, appreciating his well-timed change of the subject. We'd definitely both reached our Shark quota for the day. "I don't know about that, Tree. I may have to collect more data before I can be sure." Playfully tapping my index finger to my chin, I added, "I don't know that I've evaluated your full skill set yet. I mean, you're making a mighty huge claim here, and—"

And there I went, having to toss around a descriptor like

ANGEL PAYNE & VICTORIA BLUE

huge. Suddenly, the man was exactly that, rising from the corner seat in a move that reminded me of Godzilla's eruption from the sea. His stare was comparable, a menacing combination of so many gorgeous greens and blues. Beyond my control, mini tsunamis chased each other throughout my bloodstream.

"My skill set, hmmm?" he murmured. "Oh, I promise you haven't even scratched the surface, little girl."

I gulped. He barely noticed, closing the space between us with strides that made the water slosh. "You know, you can be very intimidating when you want to be. Has anyone ever told you that? Okay, wait." I held my hand out. "Don't answer that. There are only so many Lacis and Stacis I can stomach hearing about."

He grabbed my hand, using the grip to move in and then press his body completely against mine. My breath stuttered. My heartbeat careened. My skin was hot and sensitive, aware of every inch where he was hard yet slippery against me. With my free hand, I stroked up to his shoulder, hyperaware of how I was dripping all over him. How I instantly yet completely yearned to be dripping around other parts of him . . .

He didn't stop pushing in.

He kept going, continuing closer and harder, until I was bent backward, over the spa's outside edge. When my torso was all but splayed flat, he leaned down with me until he could speak right beside my ear. "What's this? Jealousy from the formidable Rio Katrina? My, my. I didn't think that was possible."

He stood up tall, and I quickly followed suit, trying to push him back with my free hand so I could catch my breath. The action was pointless because he easily captured my other wrist and then held them between us, even while I tossed my head back and stabbed him with a cutting laugh.

"Are you kidding? With a bedpost that has as many notches as yours? I think a girl would have to be numb not to feel at least a twinge of the stuff."

I yanked my arms back, trying to get free from his grip, but got nowhere. Grant tightened his hold, curling his hands in so mine ended up against the sculpted slabs of his pecs, and I could feel the air he pushed in and out of his flaring nostrils.

Instantly, anxiety clawed at my chest, but I tried to tamp it down. I knew Grant was playing around, and if I told him to stop, he would. At some point, though, I was going to have to get over this nonsense about him holding my hands or arms without flashing back to when he told me about Sean's accident.

"A twinge, huh?" His gaze intensified, belying distinct energy. Aroused force. I swore I could even smell it on him, and I wasn't surprised. The man had never been coy about his need to be in charge, and I'd been increasingly happy to let him try it with me. After his long and stressful dunk back into the Sebastian Shark tank, it made sense that he craved a default dive back to the waters where he controlled all the tides.

See? He was aroused. I was aroused. Everyone was having fun here.

"Yeah, just a little." I went for a careless shrug, but I knew he wasn't buying it, so I really poured it on. "You know . . . a tiny, itty-bitty bit. Not too much, though. I mean . . ." I pulled at his hold again, gritting my teeth in frustration when he wouldn't budge. "I wouldn't want your head to swell up even more."

I couldn't do it.

I couldn't take it.

Not. For. One. More. Second.

"Let go," I said through gritted teeth and made one last feeble attempt to pull my arms—my hands—hell, I didn't even know anymore—free from Grant's grasp while my entire body began to quake. Next would be a blood-curdling shriek if he didn't pick up on the way I was unraveling.

Thank God he did, though.

"Blaze." He nearly choked my name and dropped my hands simultaneously. Then he stepped toward me at the exact same time I stepped back.

"No. Stop."

How had we gotten to the Inglewood prep kitchen?

I swung my head from side to side. No. No. I tried to calm myself. We were still on the yacht. I looked around frantically, taking in details of my surroundings. Yes! We were definitely on the deck of the yacht.

But that sound... my God... what was that sound?

I could feel Grant's stare boring into the side of my face, so I shifted my stance to square off with him. All the while, a thousand different thoughts banged around inside my head. Like dirty pigeons in a city park, all taking flight in unison after a wayward child escaped his mother's grasp to terrorize them. Cacophonous, leathery wings flapped in thirty-six different directions inside my skull—all at the same time. I had to close my eyes and try to make the clamoring riot stop. With fingers pressed to my temples and eyes squeezed shut, I hummed as loudly as possible to drown out the sound.

"God! That sound—make it stop!" I looked to my hero for assistance, but he was frozen in horror too. He usually fixed everything else, but he just stood staring at me in panic.

"Make it stop!" I shouted again, gripping feverishly at my ears.

"Rio!" Grant shouted while trying to wrestle my hands down to my sides. What had started as a simple stress stopper, with my fingertips on the pressure points at my temples, had morphed into gauging at my hairline with my fingernails. Droplets of blood trickled down my face, under my jaw, and continued down my neck.

"Rio, stop! You're hurting yourself!" Grant begged.

"Make it stop!" I shouted blindly. My vision was blurry, and that damn noise!

"Baby, please! Look at me! Open your eyes and see me."

When I finally followed his commands, nothing made sense. The panicked look on his face was the most confusing of all. Jesus Christ, what just happened? My head was throbbing and hurting so badly. I carefully touched the source of the stinging sensation, only to pull back bloodstained fingertips. I shot my questioning look to Grant, but he was frozen with shock and dismay. He stared at me like I was a complete lunatic. And I'd seen the look before. I was definitely interpreting it correctly.

News flash: It never got easier.

But when the man you loved looked at you that way, a piece of your heart actually shattered.

Shit. I wasn't *in* love with Grant. That's not what I meant. I knew that. But I did love him. He represented all the good things in my life. All the things that grounded me and kept me fighting for the next day. Fighting for hope for a better day the following day.

Was I revealing all that in my gaze now too? Because when I finally built up the courage to search for his gaze again, I found it filled with nothing but sincere understanding and patience. His ocean blues were mesmerizing with their adoration, especially as he zeroed more of that energy in on me.

Oh, God.

I didn't deserve this from him. Any of it. Not ever, really, but especially right now.

The more I let my insecurities run wild in my fucked-up, broken-down mind, the more I thought what I saw was really pity. "Why are you looking at me like that?" I snapped.

"Let me help you. Or more like, can you help me right now, Blaze?" He reached for my hand, and before I could think to pull away from him, he scooped it up in his own and towed me to the closest lounge chair.

We shared the bottom half of the chaise where Grant arranged us so we faced one another. Finally, he reverently kissed the center of my palm and then pressed it to the side of his face. His skin was always so warm and virile, and he let his eyes drift closed like he was getting some sort of comfort from my touch. Could that even be possible? Could I give anything to this incredible soul? Add anything to his world when all I seemed to do was take from him? Drain him of his kindness, energy, and light?

Without taking my hand from his face, he reached for my other one and repeated the gesture. I held his handsome features between my palms, and he rubbed his stubbled cheeks between the two.

"Wha-What are you doing?" I whispered, enraptured with watching our bodies restore one another.

"Mmmm." He hummed low in his throat. "I just want to feel you touching me right now. I need to feel you. Sometimes the need is so strong I can't think of anything else but feeling your hands on me, just like this."

I rubbed small circles on his angular cheekbones with my thumbs, and he leaned into my touch even more.

"Your touch calms me or something. I don't know. It's hard to explain. I just know how I feel. And it's not a sexual thing. It feels more like a spiritual thing, as lame as that sounds." He squinted his eyes, and I was utterly floored by his honesty.

"It's not lame. It's beautiful. I'm honored to be able to give you something you need, Grant. You give me so much, so often. If this is something I can do for you—something that makes you feel good—then I'm more than happy to do it. It's not like touching you is a hardship." I laughed a little, trying to lighten the heavy conversation.

"I'm terrified you're going to vanish before my very eyes," he said, looking directly into my soul.

"And that would be a bad thing?"

"Rio . . ."

His honesty gave me the courage needed to take the final leap that he had been waiting for. Though honestly, I felt more like sprinting for the rail and diving into the ocean instead. "I'll go talk to someone when we get home," I muttered quietly. I found his gaze in the dim light of the moon and held it, waiting for the impact of my declaration to wash over him.

Grant's eyes widened, and he sat forward. It might have even been comical to watch as an outsider. Unfortunately, I just felt worse for how badly he wanted me to do this one thing. And how equally badly I didn't want to do the same thing.

"You really will?" he asked with an eagerness he didn't try to disguise.

"Shit, Tree. Don't look so enthusiastic. You're going to make me paranoid you've been thinking I'm a crackpot all this time, and you've just taken pity on me." I gave him a playful side-eye, but I knew in my heart I meant every single word.

Of course, he saw right through it. "You listen to me, Rio. Katrina. Gibson." With each part of my name, he moved deeper into my personal space. He crowded in until we were chest to chest and there wasn't room for a playing card between us.

"The only thing I've ever thought about you is how incredibly smart, funny, brave, kind, and—fuck me—sexy as hell you are. Am I making myself clear, woman?"

I just gulped and nodded. The sultry way he was looking at me now, and grinding his very hard dick into me, robbed me of any sort of coherent thought.

"So do you trust me now, Rio? I've never hurt you, have I? Everything and anything I've ever done where you're concerned has been with your best interest at the front and center. Has it not?"

"Yes. Yes, of course, it has."

"And do you trust me? I didn't miss that you left that answer out the first time," he said with a wink.

"I do," I answered solemnly.

"I really think talking to someone will help you, baby. I wouldn't lead you into something that I thought would bring you harm. Do you believe me when I say that too?"

I pulled in a long breath on purpose. He needed to see that this challenge was harder to answer than his others. And hello, talk about a buzzkill. This fit the bill way too well. On the few occasions I'd given mental health professionals a whirl, it had never been a great experience.

Finally, I did answer him. "I do," I said, looking past my magnificent Tree and out toward the horizon. We had stayed up so late at that point, the sun would soon rise to meet us head-on as we cruised home toward California. It would be glorious, and I'd probably be a little sadder.

My next thought already stacked more sadness on top of that anticipation. I had to face the question Grant wasn't asking. Perhaps the most important question of all.

Was I really ready to tackle Project Fix Rio when we got home? Was I willing to break out, open up, and fully trust people besides him with all the filthy treasures in my uncertain mind?

Looking at the hopeful expression on the devoted man's face left me with the only answer there really was. There really could be.

It was either get my shit together or lose Grant completely.

CHAPTER ELEVEN

GRANT

As Rio pulled free from me to move across the deck and slump into a chair of her own with a quiet sigh, I acknowledged the similar plummet of my heart in my chest.

Her mental health snaps, no matter the magnitude, had a way of bringing us closer together while driving us further apart. This one hadn't been the worst, not by any means, but witnessing the woman I loved, tearing at her own flesh in a fit of madness ... Shit. It gutted me on a level I couldn't fathom—especially when I had to yell at her to stop.

I was having trouble forgetting it, even several minutes later. The moment had been different from her vapor lock at the restaurant in Honolulu or even when she'd called me in gauzy, drug-influenced confusion from New Horizons. My mind cartwheeled, wondering how far she would have gotten tonight with those self-inflicted welts had I not been able to yank her back to reality.

While I'd never have that definitive answer, I could vow one thing with certainty. No way in hell would I abandon her now. Not after learning, with glaring clarity, the degree to which she needed me. A degree I didn't even know existed.

Having a woman as complex as Rio in my life was a challenge. But she was also the most exciting, most welcomed breath of fresh air I'd ever had in my life. So if that meant with the unpredictability and complexity of her vibrant personality came a few challenges, then we'd just have to face those together. As strange as it sounded, part of her enthralling magic was her confounding madness. Without one, the other wouldn't exist. As she once so eloquently told me, I saw her everything—all her parts. For that same reason, I loved her, too. All I hoped was that eventually, when she reassembled the puzzle pieces of her life that were currently so broken, there would be an open space left shaped like me.

Of course, she didn't always make it easy. Frankly, she could be downright infuriating. Like in quiet but confusing moments just like this.

"So what else did Sebastian say?"

Okay, scratch confusing. I moved straight on to perplexed, hoping she wasn't trying to toss aside the strangeness of five minutes ago with the oddest of subject changes. But damn it, why else would she bring up Bas, of all people?

Fuck.

We were doing so well too. She was really listening to me—or so I'd thought. She seemed to be actually absorbing everything I said, including the praise she found so hard to accept unless we were burning up the bedsheets. If that were only the case now. I yearned to groan aloud from frustration. We only had a couple nights left under the ocean's starry sky before we would be back in LA. I wanted to be naked with my firestorm as much as possible until then.

"Why the hell are you asking that now?" I answered her in a dangerously low but thoroughly unintentional register. But hell, did I thank myself for it. At once, her demeanor shifted. She rubbed her thighs together by subtle inches, and her eyes grew glassed with arousal.

"I don't understand," she muttered. "Why wouldn't I ask it?"

"Because you don't actually care about Sebastian Shark, and you know it," I challenged.

"Says you and what jury?"

"Says me, period. And my bullshit meter is pegged in the red zone with all the crap you're dishing out, woman." I made sure to lock eyes with her for the next part. "So, tell me what's really going on in that beautiful mind of yours, or I'll make sure you can't sit down for a week—and it won't be from a spanking."

Yeah, distracting her with sex was a dirty tactic, but I didn't want to have a minute more of heavy conversation tonight. I was seriously done with it—even without the reminder from my groin, growing stiffer as I watched her there in the moonlight.

And then stiffer still, as Rio claimed restorative gulps of oxygen. Dear God, she was the most alluring female I'd ever known—especially as she kept processing my threat while focusing her brown sugar stare on me.

"This isn't bullshit, Grant. I'm serious."

I frowned. "About discussing Sebastian?"

"About discussing what you've given up with him—for me." She blinked, and the glass in her stare turned into a more troubling sheen. "I don't want to watch you continue to destroy a lifelong friendship like you've been doing. Please . . . how can I help make this right? Just because I loathe the man doesn't mean—"

"Blaze." I stood so abruptly, she startled. Visually, she followed my short journey until I stood before where she was huddled on the chair. She gave a little yelp when I scooped her up and dropped down on the luxurious cushion myself and arranged her little body on my lap.

"Okay," I finally asked when she was tucked beneath my chin. "What's all this really all about?"

Her sigh, though practically ponderous, spread some welcome warmth across my chest. "It's about... setting things right."

"And now I'm really lost."

"Setting things right." She emphasized that by jabbing a finger directly over my heart. "When we get back, I want to do what I should've done right after the accident. I'm going to go and tell Shark what happened. Exactly how that fire at the Edge's job site got started. If he wants to press charges, then that's his prerogative. I wasn't strong enough to do it then, but I think I can deal with the consequences now."

I pulled back a little, studying her for a long time. Finally, I decided it might be best to humor her. Maybe if she got the idea completely off her chest, she'd let it go.

"Can I ask what's changed? I mean, why now? Elijah went through a lot of trouble to clean and cover up the mess at the site that night. Not to mention, he and I have been lying to Sebastian ever since. So, to just go to Bas now..." And suddenly, I wasn't indulging her anymore. Once I brought up Elijah, I realized that I couldn't. This was much bigger than just some tension between Bas and me. "Shit," I muttered. "I don't know, baby. This could really cause more harm than good."

"What is the right thing to do, then?" Deep concern twisted her beautiful face. "What will make all of this better? I'm terrified I'm going to lose you, Grant. If that were to happen?" Rio sucked air between her teeth in a gasp that sounded painful. "I . . . I would be completely devastated. And I won't survive that state of mind again. I'd go back to the way I was right after the accident. Those first few days, I was a shell of myself, Grant. I can't do that again. I just can't."

She held my hands so tightly her knuckles were visibly white, even in the darkest part of the night.

Her whole body shuddered with the memory. Her conflict and agony were so palpable, I almost gave in to the same kind of tremors.

After forcing down a pair of thorough breaths, thankful when the briny air scoured my senses back to calmness, I pulled her even tighter to my chest. It was a rare occurrence when this fierce firestorm showed any type of vulnerability—to anyone—and I wanted to give her, and this moment, the deserved recognition.

Easily, I maneuvered her in my arms so she faced me. Because she was on my lap, our noses were nearly touching. "Look right at me while I say this, Blaze. All of it." I waited for her to focus on my eyes, getting past her normal fidgeting. Staying centered was more challenging for her than most, but I would wait. Always for her, I'd wait.

I dipped my head in, really studying her. "You with me, baby?"

She breathed in. I breathed out. Perfect synchronicity. As it always had been. As I desperately wished it always would be.

"I'm not going to leave you, okay? I won't unless you tell me to go, and even then, I still might not do it." I gave her a playful wink along with the grin guaranteed to make her pussy wet—every time. Though this time, arguably, it mattered the most. "I want to be with you, Rio. I thought I had made this clear to you by this point, but that's okay."

I lifted her hands to my lips and gently kissed the knuckles on both hands.

"Here is the part that is nonnegotiable for me, though. The part we talked about already, so it won't come as a surprise. I want you to be *happy*, but I need you to be *healthy*." I paused for a couple beats, really measuring my words. "Healthy and stable. I'm serious about the counseling, but I don't want to beat it into the ground here. I'd even be happy to go with you—or you can go alone; whatever you want, I'll support your choice. But you can't keep starting fires, Rio. You just can't."

I studied her face carefully as my words settled over the quiet night. The lapping of the water against the hull of the boat was the deceptively calm soundtrack to our conversation.

"Tree," she huffed and tried to get off my lap, but I held her closer. I had a flashback of Abbi at Kaisan's baby shower, having to do the same thing when Rio tried to pull away. The woman was a pro at this move—but now I was a pro at recognizing it.

"Listen to me, okay?" I insisted. "I know none of this is going to be easy."

She gave up a delicate snort. "And now he's the king of understatement."

"Fine. You're going to be putting in some really hard work; I don't doubt that at all. But I want to be by your side, and I want to help you get through this. The question is, will you let me?"

Several moments passed before Rio gave her head a little shake, and I watched quietly to see if she would tell me on her own or make me ask what idea thread she had tugged and then chased like an unraveling hem on a sweater.

I caved first. Damn it. "Hey. Where did your mind run off to just then?"

I asked it with a grin so she'd catch the playful nature of my inquiry. Still, she rubbed her forehead, her eyebrows pulled together in worry. "I was thinking about the last time I went to therapy."

I pushed together my own brows. "How long ago was that?"

"A while." She was clearly not going to get more specific, so I didn't push—especially when she gave another little shake of her head and let out a miserable groan. "God, it was the worst."

"The therapist or the sessions themselves?" When she didn't answer yet again, just continuing to scowl and rub absently at her forehead, I tried a new tack. "What did you like the least about it?"

Suddenly, she jerked up her head as if I'd simply asked if she wanted a midnight snack. "You know what?" she said, gushing with forced brightness. "I'm calling a moratorium on this topic until we are back on California soil. Deal?" There was no waiting for my reply. "I want to make the absolute most of the time we have left out here on the open water. Alone. Talking about our fondest shrink memories isn't my idea of fun, Tree."

I'd give her this one. I wasn't sure if the idea of *us* was something she was ready to deal with in the real world when we got back, so I needed to get my fill of her now, while I still had the chance. Since that had been my plan several hours ago—*thanks again, Bas*—I didn't have to dig deep for a wholehearted grin of approval. Of course, her soft proximity and scantily clad curves didn't hurt either.

"A moratorium, hmm?" I drawled, finding the indent of her waist with my exploring touch. "I do love it when you use

GRANT'S FLAME

those big, fancy words, Ms. Blaze."

"My words aren't the shit that should be big and impressive right now, Mr. Twombley."

Well, damn. No arguing with that one either. As our mouths found each other, stoking our desires higher with teasing, tentative nips and tugs, I finally dared to murmur, "So do you want to ride me under the stars tonight, Blaze? Or do you want to go back to our ca—oh shit!"

I interrupted myself with a grateful groan from the second she reached into my bathing suit, boldly grabbing at my stiff shaft. Rio smiled softly against my lips, offering the sweet deliverance of her own aroused moan.

"Now here's what I call big."

I managed half a laugh before losing my voice—and probably half my mind—to a surge of hot stimulation. Scalding pressure pumped up from my balls and spurted across her fingers in anticipatory drops. "Baby, that feels so good. Yes. Squeeze me tighter. Yesss…"

Her small hand felt divine wrapped around me. After a little guidance, she gripped with the perfect amount of pressure, and I swore I saw angels dancing in the stars. But if she kept up with the wondrous torture, I'd be finished before we barely started. I allowed myself to enjoy the pleasure for another minute before surging abruptly to my feet and then glaring down at my little woman. And yes, it was definitely a glare. Capitulating to a tender regard meant I'd likely come right here in my trunks. Not acceptable. Not right now. I needed this authority. And she sure as fuck needed to give it to me.

"You still with me?" I demanded, absorbing the new shine of her perusing, adoring gaze. Thankfully, her reply was fast and eager.

"Oh yes. Very much so."

"Good," I stated. "Undress."

She looked up with a lust-drunk stare, but that was it. She made no motion toward doing my bidding. Even the wind, picking up the ends of my hair, did nothing to move hers.

"Rio," I warned. "If I count you down, you'll be sorry, girl."

Her playful pout disintegrated. "Grant!" she cried. "No, damn it! I'm doing it, I'm doing it. Fuck, I hate that stupid threat. I wish you'd never started that."

"Yes, but look at how effective it is, my stubborn little mule."

I chuckled, pinching her nipples the second she removed her bikini top. Damn, it felt good to pull that one out of my arsenal again. We were fooling around a few days prior, in a situation much like this, and she'd decided to put on her favorite feisty face. Since she was channeling her inner toddler, I happily pulled out my inner disciplinarian, complete with the countdown. I'd been secretly delighted when she actually chose to test me about the follow-through. She'd learned about orgasm edging the hard way that day—though I strongly hoped, for both our sakes, that wouldn't be the case tonight.

While she reached down to push down her bathing suit bottoms too, I kept my attention on her stunning, pert breasts. Good fuck, they were works of art. As my lust swelled, my touch grew rougher. I skimmed my palms over her again and again, savoring how the pretty tips stood to firm points for me. I kept up the treatment, pulling and plucking as her breathing doubled and her skin got dewy. I loved watching her like this. Needing me as much as I craved her. Knowing we were both going to get exactly what we wanted. Soon ... so very soon ...

"Now come here." I held my hand out, and she trustingly

placed her palm in mine. I brought her fingers to my lips and kissed each one in turn, starting with her thumb. When I got to her pinky, I made my way back, this time sucking thoroughly on each one. Throughout each moment, I held her aroused stare captive with mine.

Just when her gaze reached its hottest, heaviest zenith, I surprised her by tugging hard so her body lurched toward me. In nearly the same motion, I quickly wrapped my arm around her waist, swept her off her feet, and laid her beneath me on the sofa.

"Jesus, Grant! Holy shit." She burst into laughter that was brighter than any star above us. My own smile nearly split my face in two. Filthy inspiration struck, and my smile turned wicked.

"Put this foot on the deck," I told her, tapping the leg closest to me. "And put this one up over the back of the sofa."

I watched her comply from my taller vantage point. I leaned back to get an even better view of her widely spread pussy and nearly came from just looking at the perfect, erotic sight.

"Holy mother of God," I muttered, my voice like torched shrubbery. I cleared my throat—well, tried to—and boosted my volume so my fire starter could hear me too. "You're so damn sexy, my perfect Blaze. I wish you could see how hot you look right now."

"Hmm." She writhed and smiled, nearly gouging my heart from my chest with her irresistible allure. "Guess I'll have to take your word for it."

"My God. I think I've fucking died and gone to heaven."

The urge to feel her skin—to experience the silky, creamy perfection beneath my fingertips—was as strong as a siren's song to wayward sailors. But I wanted to build her anticipation for her just a little longer, so I got busy with my own flesh instead. While I praised her perfection with grunts and groans worthy of the watery abyss over which we glided, I reached into my trunks and grabbed my cock. I didn't go easy on myself. I jerked myself fiercely, punishing my flesh from balls to crown, using the new spurts of my precome as lubricant.

"When I get my fingers in you, baby, and then my cock? You're going to feel me in your throat."

Rio gulped hard. "Promise?"

"Hell yeah, I promise. You know why? Because you've been such a good girl for me tonight. You're spread open so wide, I'm going to be able to get in this pussy so deep."

Rio whimpered in time to the tremble of her thighs, the aroused hitches of her breaths. "Grant, please."

"What, my love?"

"Stop teasing. Please. Make me feel good."

Slowly, I leaned over, pressing my lips close to her ear. "Now, listen to me, sweet Rio." I nibbled her earlobe, and she moaned with more force. "Everyone on this boat is sleeping right now, and I'm about to do things to this perfect body that will make you want to scream louder than you thought possible." As I growled the rest of my intentions into her ear, her breathing rate increased and became erratic.

"Grant!"

I broadened my smile before answering serenely, "Yes, dear?"

"Please! Just...just... I'll be quiet, okay?"

"All right, then. But Blaze..."

"What?" she snapped.

"If I hear so much as a peep from you, I'll have to stop."

She nodded with frenetic speed. "Not a peep," she rasped. "Just please, don't stop. Okay? I'll be so good. Gr—"

I couldn't hold back any longer. I kissed her passionately, celebrating the hot slide of our tongues against each other, before my mind made its inexorable shift to other wet recesses of her delicious body. Couldn't hold back my need for that either. With a sound of animalistic greed, I reached down and slid my middle finger between the swollen cushions at her apex. Beyond them was the nirvana of her tight, sweet channel.

I drove in with fervent purpose. Then again. And again. Farther each time. Rejoicing in every primal, virulent thrust— then stopped. I kept my finger deep within her body but didn't provide friction, just fullness. However, I emulated the rhythm with the force of my lips on hers, pumping her mouth with my tongue instead. I didn't let up with the carnal kissing until I was certain my whole hand was coated in her slickness, and when she moaned, I swallowed the mesmerizing sound down my throat.

"Quiet, baby. Remember?" I broke away from her mouth to move down her neck, kissing and licking the sensitive skin as I went. But within a few minutes, when I pulled back to observe my woman's state of arousal, her eyebrows were once more drawn together in frustration. This time, the sight had me holding back a chuckle. I liked this version of her scowl much better than before. No, I was actually fascinated by it. For several long moments, I watched the different techniques she employed to get her own satisfaction from my practically stationary finger, all while trying to remain stealthy about it.

But it didn't take her long to grow tired of the wriggling. "Grant…"

I cut off her plea with another, more aggressive, kiss.

It was full and brutal and possessive, a devouring thing with greedy lips and tongue. It was the sort of kiss that reminded her I would take her to the highest heights and then catch her when she plummeted over the edge to incredible ecstasy too.

And while I did that, I gave her what she wanted so badly. More.

More anything. More everything.

I pulled my finger out but immediately slid two back in. That way, the sensation assaulting her pussy was uniform.

"Mmmm." I hummed in appreciation of my view. Watching her sex devour my fingers like a hungry mouth was utterly pornographic. "How's that, Blaze?" I taunted. "Better? Are you full now, sweetheart? Is that what you needed?"

At first, she didn't respond. Or perhaps couldn't. Yeah, I liked that idea. "More, Grant," she whimpered, her chest pumping hard to get it out. "Please. More! Feels ... so good ..."

I crooked my fingers lightly along the top of her channel while slowly pulling out. Then, just before leaving heaven altogether, I straightened both fingers and thrust back in. It was much like I'd do with my cock. I was damn sure she realized that too, if I was reading her lusty expression correctly. And damn, did I want to ready every syllable of this woman before scrambling her back up like my own sexual Scrabble board. What new words would I create with her crooning consonants, her sighing vowels? What incredible depths had I yet to discover inside her?

I couldn't wait to find out. To go even deeper, right the fuck now—but my quest to explore her very center was stopped by my knuckles banging against her untried asshole. Untried by me, at least.

And there was a thought best left alone at this moment,

unless I planned on blowing my wad from the sheer force of imagination.

Instead, I focused on anchoring my writhing woman to the sofa with one forearm banded across her abdomen, as I continued the taunting circuit repeatedly. Every time, Rio dug her short fingernails into my flesh while I spun her out of control with desire. Slick, hot plentitudes of it.

"Christ, can you hear how wet you are?" I asked in a low growl. "After you come for me, I'm going to make a feast out of all of this sweet juice, baby. I mean, just look at the mess you're making."

I leaned over her, holding my shiny, sticky fingers between our faces.

"You see that? It's all from you, Rio. Taste yourself, baby." I put my flat palm closer to her mouth then and instructed, "Lick."

I was entranced by the sight of her cleaning my finger with her talented pink tongue. She made erotic swipes up and down each side until I closed the space between our faces and joined her. With my own tongue, I washed my finger too, meeting Rio's tongue to twirl and stroke my digit between us. Our licking and sucking grew to fevered intensity, and I had to either taste her pussy directly from the source or fuck her. Either one, but I would embarrass myself and come in my shorts if I didn't make a move.

"Good girl," I crooned. "But now, let me back in this cunt, woman." I moved back down her body, and my hands went right to the treasure between her legs. I toyed with her like that for a while, entranced with the gorgeous textures of her swollen clit and labia, before I gave in to temptation once again—and leaned in to take them with a tender kiss.

"Oh, God!" Rio blurted. "Grant...ohhhh!"

"Good, baby?" I queried, halfway serious. "Yeah?"

"I don't know," she gasped, thrashing her head against the cushions. For an extended second, feeling like the world's luckiest voyeur, I simply watched her. I envisioned what we must look like from the stars, with her spread for me like a carnal feast. The only thing better about the vision would be me fucking her like the animal I now felt like. "I...I don't know!" she repeated, voice rising with her exigency.

"Quiet," I reminded quickly.

Her next words were instantly softer. "It's so sensitive. It's...it's so...It feels...I feel like I'm going to come in one minute."

"And that's a bad thing?"

I chuckled it out, letting her feel the vibrations along the insides of her thighs. Though I was being snarky and hypothetical, I almost expected her comeback anyway. She didn't say a word, opting to grab my hair in both hands and hold my head between her legs. I finished her off in a little more than the minute she'd estimated, but I gave her a pass on the poor guess.

She galloped across the finish line with one of my large hands covering her mouth and the other very busy between her legs, finger fucking her like a madman. All the while, I sucked and licked that precious pink paradise like it was the last time I would ever have the chance.

"Holy shit, Grant Twombley," she stammered out a few minutes later, still trying to even out her breathing. "What has gotten into you tonight?"

"As opposed to last night?"

She smacked my shoulder. "You know what I mean."

"Or the one before that?"

"That was..." Then she rolled her head over as if I'd returned the playful nudge. "Shit, that was just..."

I chuckled softly. "I'm obsessed with you. I can't help it." I buried my face in her neck and sucked her sweat-slicked skin. "I need more. Need to be inside you, Rio."

"Well, what are you waiting for?" she asked with a challenging look.

"Hmm." I pondered. "Perhaps... a new view."

"Huh?"

"Kneel." I patted the cushion of the sofa. "Face the back." If we didn't break this piece of furniture after this, it would be a miracle. "I'm in the mood for a rough ride, Blaze. Can you take it? Can you stay quiet?"

"Just stick your dick in me, Tree. Let me worry about the rest." She rolled her head, grabbed the back of the sofa, and faced forward. Her position put her sweet little ass in the perfectly vulnerable place for a spank after that sassy remark. I followed the first swat with a few more, in case she considered being that bratty again.

"Grant!" she shouted.

"Quiet," I hissed. "Or there will absolutely be more where that came from." I meant it completely, especially as I drank in my visual fill of her. "Christ. Look how pretty this ass is with my handprint on it."

Roughly, I rubbed the blooming red mark deeper into her flesh. Rio replied with a long, lush moan from behind her pressed lips. The sound of her whimpers, blending with the night wind, formed a tent in my shorts as painful as it was prominent.

"Christ," I grated. "I seriously didn't think my dick could

get any harder than it was."

But remarkably, the prolonged sight of her perfect backside did just that. I stroked my hand down her back, fighting to be smooth and masterful, before sliding my fingers between her legs and finding her perfect, sensitive spot.

"Fuck, baby, this wet cunt is killing me." I pushed a couple fingers in, and she gasped.

"God, yes. So good!" Rio pushed her bottom back, and I slid a third finger into her slick, sweet hole. "Fuuuck," she hissed, though the sound approached another audible explosion. "I'm trying to be quiet. I swear I am!"

I leaned over, pressing my chest against her back, before saying against her ear, "Do I need to gag you, Blaze? I'm sure I can come up with something around here to do it with."

Her walls convulsed tighter around my fingers. I should've been happy with that, but I tempted fate even more by ruthlessly turning my hand over to again stimulate her G-spot.

"Grant!" She was still at a whisper but barely clung to the control. Urgency changed the octave of her voice and turned her breaths into stuttering puffs. "D-Don't do that. Please…"

"But baby, doesn't it feel so good?" I blatantly teased. "You know it does." I bit solidly into the side of her neck, which had her sucking in more shaky air through her nostrils. "I'm going to keep fingering you like this for as long as I damn well please. And you're going to take every second of it, baby, and you're going to love it. Then I'm going to ram my big cock inside you, and you're going to fucking love that more."

More shuddering pants, sawing in and out of her lips. More exquisite tremors, taking over every inch of her torrid tunnel. "But… I can't stay quiet… with all that stimu—ahhh! Shit! Grant!"

"Ssshhh! Quiet!" I warned. "Do I really need to get that gag?"

"Please." She thrashed her head left to right again, doubling the pressure in my cock. How I loved taming my gorgeous little rebel. "Don't do it."

But while her lips mouthed the protest, she pushed her pussy onto my hand harder and harder with each inward stroke. Hastily, I looked around, and—*Bingo*. The T-shirt I'd been wearing earlier was nearby, piled on the corner of the cushion. Quickly, I handed it to Rio.

"I'm not going to be gentle, baby," I growled. "So just get that through your pretty head right now and take care of the screams I'm going to give you."

With that, she immediately knew what to do with the cloth. Before I was done with my erotic promise, she stuffed a wad of the fabric into her mouth and dramatically bit down, giving me the all clear to go to town.

Thank. Fuck.

After a few more finger strokes to make sure she was perfectly primed, I shoved balls-deep into her welcoming heat. Her muffled whine was heaven. My soaring lust was paradise. It felt like I'd waited a lifetime to be inside this woman, even though we'd fucked that morning when we woke up. Ramping her up and then easing off, over and over, was as torturous for me as it was for her. By the time I finally felt her pussy caress my shaft with her unique, orgasmic pulses, my eyes were simultaneously crossing and rolling back in my head. I gave her more frenzied strokes. More grueling thrusts. At last, the dam broke. It was completely, amazingly, worth the wait. My load felt rocket-throttled up my shaft, until it burst out into the—

Holy. Mother. Of. God.

At once, I froze—not that my dick was paying any attention. It kept coming with NASA-detectable force, much to my shock, horror, and chagrin.

Damn it, damn it, *damn it.*

How the fuck had this happened?

What the fuck was I thinking?

For the first time in my entire sexually active life, I'd forgotten to put on a condom.

How had Rio not even noticed? Or said anything? After one look, I had that answer. She was lost to the ongoing waves of her own climax, her shoulders still shaking and her ass still clenching.

Jesus fucking Christ.

I didn't even know if she was on any other type of birth control. It wasn't something we'd ever talked about because I used condoms like a religious man with rosary beads.

I hated having to pull out of her body but did so quickly. Nearly in the same motion, I picked her up off the sofa. We'd address this debacle in a few minutes when the high wore off. I'd worked the girl over pretty good, and she was now on her way to utter exhaustion.

I carried her back to our cabin, where I went straight into the bathroom. While I ran the water in the shower, Rio sat on the stool by the vanity. A bath would've been ideal, but the tub was smaller than usual, and at my height, there was no way we'd both fit. I really wanted to spoil her a little more, since my own stupidity had quashed the possibility of postcoital affection up on deck.

"I'm so tired, Grant. Can't we just get into bed?" my girl whined.

"We will, I promise. I just want to clean you up first." And use the time to recollect my frenzied thoughts. "Come on." I tugged her toward the shower, despite how she dragged her feet. "In you go," I said, holding the door to the shower stall open. As soon as she got over the shallow lip, I stepped in behind her.

Rio put her hand on the middle of my chest and looked up at me with pleading eyes. "Seriously. I don't think I can go another round."

My body shook with my silent chuckle at her earnest version of rejection. "I'm not looking for another session under the shower spray, Blaze. I really just want to take care of you. Turn around and get your hair wet so I can wash it."

For the next hour, I became Deluxe Spa Grant. I washed and conditioned her hair, loofahed every inch of her delicate skin, and lovingly patted her dry when we were through. She insisted her hair would air-dry quickly, so I just combed through the tangles before massaging lotion into the front and the back of her body.

"Do you want one of my T-shirts to sleep in?" I asked while grabbing one for myself.

"Yes, please," she mumbled into the pillow but drifted off to sleep before I could even get the makeshift nightie on her.

I snorted with a quiet laugh. "And naked works too, baby," I murmured, grabbing a chance to trace adoring fingers over the curves of her profile. While my physical touch was a testament to her outer beauty, its silent progression was proxy for the trumpets of my heart and chorus of my spirit. The music that confirmed my mind's determined decision.

I was so fucking smitten with this female. And I didn't want to keep it a secret any longer. Even when we got back to LA.

Finally, I forced myself to drag away and make the nightly rounds of the stateroom. I plugged her phone in to charge, brushed my teeth, turned on the small light in the bathroom we were using as a night light, and checked the door's lock one last time before turning off the main light switch.

As soon as darkness enveloped the room, my own fatigue set in. Jesus, the woman had drained me—in all the best ways.

But just as I settled in, tucked my girl close, and finally shut my eyes, a rowdy commotion erupted on the deck above our cabin.

"What the fuck?" I kept it beneath my breath, not wanting to disturb the slumbering beauty at my side. But seriously, what the fuck? We'd been on the boat enough days and nights by then to recognize familiar sounds around us—and a herd of elephants taking a spin class above our bed was definitely not something that had happened before.

I listened, not moving, for at least another three minutes. The tromping feet intensified, joined by a lot of urgent, angry shouting.

What. The. Fuck?

Though I didn't vocalize it this time, Rio sat up and rubbed her eyes. "What's going on? It can't be morning."

"Go back to sleep, baby," I soothed. "But do me a favor and put some clothes on in case something's going on. I don't like you naked if someone barges in here. It sounds like someone's come aboard."

"What? Aren't we still really far away from land?"

"Yeah, I think so. I don't know for sure, though. There are a lot of small islands between here and the coast, but they're uninhabitable." I whispered it all, conscious that our conversation could likely be heard directly above.

"So, what the h—" Rio cut her own rasp short as new shouts erupted above. Whoever it was, was very angry. My experience with both our yacht crews, for the journey to Hawaii as well as this leg, had only been pleasant. The aggressive vibe from this overheard exchange did not line up with anything I had experienced.

Shit.

Something wasn't right.

And damn it, I didn't feel safe leaving Rio alone in the cabin to go investigate.

"For fuck's sake, Blaze, I said get dressed like ten minutes ago. I'm serious," I said tersely when I noticed she still hadn't moved from the bed.

"I was trying to listen," she retorted, pointed up toward the ceiling. "And I didn't want to make noise." She went to the dresser and yanked a pair of pajama bottoms from one of the drawers, and I crossed the room to her while she tugged them on.

Taking my T-shirt from her trembling fingers, I waited for her to look up at me. "Don't be scared."

"I'm not."

"Then why are you shaking?"

A shrug, fast but telling. "Tired, I guess."

I narrowed my eyes and helped her slide into my shirt. We both knew that excuse was bullshit, but now wasn't the time to get into it further. I bent low, kissed the tip of her nose, and then tugged her back to the bed.

"In you go, my love. Let's worry about all the drama on deck when the sun rises. You wore me out, sex fiend."

She giggled, and I was positive it was my favorite sound on the entire planet. My own smile started as a grin but kept spreading across my face like a run in a woman's pantyhose. It went from one side to the other in no time, and there was no explanation of how it had happened.

"All right, Tree," she said, scooting down into the covers. "What's the big, cheesy smile about?"

"Oh, that's all your fault." I smoothed the blankets up to her chin and then sat on the bed's side by her shoulder.

Rio gazed up at me with her big brown eyes. In the dim light, her pupils were overtaking her irises, making her look even more like a porcelain doll than usual. So exquisite. So breathtaking. So mine. I couldn't fight the conclusions anymore. I didn't even want to.

"My fault?" Her smile broadened too. "How so?"

"It's so good to hear you giggle. Not just laugh, Rio, but no shit"—I shook my head while grinning again—"*giggle*. Music to my ears."

Her grin faded a little, but not in the way that usually made my gut clench. Just the opposite. Despite her sudden seriousness, my senses were lighter.

"Music," she repeated, as if I'd just spouted a whole poem for her. "Really?"

"Really," I affirmed, gliding a soft touch between her chin and the blanket. The strange scuffling across the boat had my protective instincts—and the need to show them—cranking to new highs. "Baby, your happiness is more important—"

But I never had a chance to finish the thought.

Our cabin's door banged open like a shotgun opened fire on the thing from the other side.

The panel flew so wildly, one of the hinges tore from the short screws holding it in place, causing it to hang askew and grind to a halt in the carpet.

"Fuck!" I barked. At the same time, Rio let out a frightened shriek. Instinctively, I shielded her with my body, pressing her back against the bed's headboard. If someone wanted to harm my woman, they would have to go through me first.

"Twombley! Grant Twombley!"

But it wasn't her they were after.

As an unfamiliar, smarmy-looking man bellowed it again, I gulped against equal parts relief and dread. The stranger shoved past our usual porter and strode to the room's center. Three additional men pushed their way through the small doorway, all as equally dirty, determined, and demanding as the first guy.

"It's okay, baby," I said to Rio over my shoulder. "Ssshhh. It's okay."

I thrust my hand back toward her. Instantly, she took the offering. Her fingers were icicles. A bass drum pulsed at her wrist.

"Get on your fucking feet, douchebag," the greaseball barked. As he did, I noticed that one of our intruders was actually the crew member who'd shown these idiots to our cabin. He whimpered in the corner like a little rabbit circled by a pack of coyotes.

Well, shit.

If he was our only chance of escape, we were in deep trouble.

I rose with slow care, holding my hands in front of my midsection, palms open and not threatening. "Listen, buddy. I think there's been some sort of misunderstanding. I don't know who you are, but I'm sure whatever—"

"Shut the fuck up!" the first asshole swore, spit flying from his sweaty lips. "Now, nice and easy," he said, waving the barrel of his gun around as though it were a theater usher's flashlight. "Over here."

As I complied, I noticed all four of these idiots were gun-slinging, and I wasn't talking about a Daisy Red Ryder that would only be putting my eye out.

"Easy," I told them, battling to keep my face and voice completely neutral. "Easy now, boys. If it's money you're after, I can get whatever amount you—"

Again, I didn't get to finish my thought. The tallest bully cracked me in the back of the head with the butt of his weapon. The giant ape snarled when his assault didn't take me to the ground, but the dumbass didn't consider physics. My height advantage meant he would've had to hit me at either a sharper angle or with much more force to do the level of damage he hoped for. It would stand to reason that he wasn't a criminal by night and a nuclear engineer by day, however. Yeah, I figured that out even with the fucking headache I was going to have.

Damn it. Now I was really pissed.

With my anger lending a strange jolt of bravery, I turned around to size the guy up. It was likely a stupid move, but I compounded it by decking him square in the face. As he folded to his knees, his comrades swore. Their profanities were drowned as Rio let out another shriek from where she was balled up on the bed.

Quickly, I steadied my assailant's head between my palms. At the same time, I kneed him in the face. Satisfying, bone-crunching sounds pinged around the small room as blood spurted from the bastard's nostrils. A sanguine spray redecorated the cabin's light-colored carpet before he fell to the ground and rolled into the fetal position.

"Asshole," I muttered and turned to the leader of the pack.

"Stop fucking around. What do you want? You know my name. Obviously you came here with something specific in mind."

The guy forced a laugh. As if he came straight from central casting, he was missing a couple of crucially located teeth. "Well, shit," he drawled. "They did say you were a no-nonsense kind of guy."

"Really? And who are they?"

"Doesn't matter," he hedged. "Really doesn't matter."

At once, I was brutally tempted to sprawl him to the floor, as well. But I held back, boring grooves into my palms with my fingernails. Taking him down wouldn't be wise. My every instinct was telling me so.

"Again, what do you want?" I demanded. "Money? A favor from someone I know? Although if you staged this whole thing"—I waved my arm around—"attacking a private boat out in the middle of open water, someone with pretty deep pockets must be bankrolling you."

"Again, doesn't matter."

Fucking God, I was really tired of this guy's grandstanding. I re-entertained the idea of flattening him. Judging by the looks of the two other thugs, I could probably take them out myself, as well. It would be tough if they ganged up on me, but if I could tangle with one at a time, I stood a pretty good chance of them all staying unconscious for a bit. At least long enough for Rio to get out of this cabin alive.

"Last time, asshole. What. Do. You. Want?" I taunted.

The nasty guy gave a careless shrug. "You, of course."

CHAPTER TWELVE

RIO

In a flash, I was on my feet and ready to stand guard in front of Grant. The man I needed like air. The man who picked me up and dusted me off—time and time again. I'd be damned if I'd sit by and have another man I loved ripped from my life.

Hell no.

I'd fight tooth and nail to keep him safe and have no regrets about doing it, regardless of how I had to do it.

Because that's what he would do for me.

That's what he had done for me.

"Fuck you, scumbag!" I surged forward even more, shouting it at the creepy guy who appeared to be the leader of this pile of trash that had commandeered our room. My bravado was fueled by an intense fear that threatened to take over my whole mind. If Grant were to leave with these men? I'd lose him forever. The chances of seeing him alive again weren't good.

No. They were straight up shitty.

Grant whirled on me in a heartbeat and gripped my shoulders in his strong palms. Leaning in so his lips were a hairbreadth from my ear, he said, "Blaze, I need you to listen to me." He pulled back to scrutinize me and then got right back in my face after the briefest moment. "For Christ's sake," he huffed. "Nod or say something so I know I'm getting through to you. We don't have the luxury of time right now."

I couldn't blame the man for losing patience with me, given the harrowing situation. Now wasn't the time for me to become a deer-in-headlights on him.

With a deep inhale, I gave a quick dip of my chin. But apparently, that wasn't convincing enough. I needed to show him a glimpse of the warrior I knew was deep inside. I needed to fight alongside this brave man for once, instead of letting him take the brunt of all the shit storms that rained down on us. There wouldn't be whimpering in the corner, acting helpless, and then apologizing for it later. This was Grant's freedom at stake, and I couldn't let these bastards take him from me.

"I'm listening," I said quietly but steadily.

"Thank you." He laid the gentlest kiss on my forehead before leveling his intense blue stare to mine. "Okay. Listen to me," he gritted. "I don't know what these douchebags want, but if they insist I go with them, I'm going to do it."

I gasped. "No!"

"Yes," he insisted. "It's the only way, baby—especially if it means you'll remain safe on this boat. But the second we leave and you have a cell signal, call Bas and Elijah."

Undoubtedly, my eyes flared wide with rage at the mere mention of Sebastian fucking Shark's name. Grant, clearly already prepared for my reaction, wrapped me in his arms and gripped my nape with one of his huge hands.

"Put that shit aside, Rio. He will be one of two people who will be able to help. I have little doubt this has something to do with him anyway. It always does. So call him. If he's the problem, let him be the solution."

He drifted off with his comment, but I heard every word

since we were in a tight embrace. My blood pressure spiked at the sickening knowledge I was probably going to lose another piece of my heart because of that selfish bastard. I gulped hard, barely holding in a cavalcade of anguished sobs.

"All right, enough with the lover's bullshit. Twombley, you're coming with us, whether you like it or not." The gang leader's gravelly voice was like pouring water on a grease fire to my already ramped-up consternation. Then the slimeball continued, "Do it under your own will, or we'll find ways of taking your will from you. Actually, that part might be kind of fun."

He laughed, igniting a round of raucous laughter with his creepy cronies. Even the asshole Grant had kneed in the nose was back on his feet and very angry. Though he was holding our bathroom towel to his face, he still wanted his pound of flesh. His voice was nasally when he added, "Ways we'd enjoy very much."

Number three held up his index finger while pointing out, "Boss said we had to deliver him without a hair out of place." He quickly lowered his hand, though, when the others spat their disapproving reactions.

"Fuck that!" the bloody guy bellowed. "That was before he did this!" He held up the towel to remind his mate of the hit he'd taken.

By-The-Rules shrugged. "Well, I'm not going to be the one to piss off the boss. I just want my money when this is done."

I couldn't stay quiet any longer. "Is this all about money? If you want money, I'll get your money. And who is this boss you keep mentioning? I'll double what you're getting from your big bad boss if you just get off this boat now and leave us alone. We can forget this ever happened."

Grant stepped in front of me, blocking my view of the entire cabin. He took a few steps back, moving us both toward the bed until I bumped into the mattress with the backs of my legs, and he felt my body halt behind him. It was only then that he turned around to face me.

He bent low to speak for my ears only. "Baby, listen to me. I appreciate the effort and the offer, but I don't want you to call attention to yourself again. Okay?" He only waited for a beat or two for my reply, and when it didn't come, he continued. "We don't know how long these creeps have been out to sea, and scumbags like these have very little, if anything, to lose." He gave me a brief hug that felt more like desperation, and then after only a moment, he jerked me away from his body.

I could only guess it was to gauge my reaction to what he had said. But my face was twisted in confusion as I tried to follow whatever path he was leading us down with his weird comments.

My dearest let out an exasperated breath and spewed, "I don't want to have to watch you get gang-raped by four fucking pirates right before they drag me out of here to beat me an inch from my life because of some fucking debt someone is trying to collect of Sebastian's. Is that clear enough?"

"Very," I croaked, feeling like I was going to vomit. "Grant." I pleaded with my eyes while I begged with my words. "Please, please don't give in. I can't… I can't do this without you." A wave of my hand around the room symbolized the word this, meaning life, in my declaration.

But I had to continue. If this was the one and only chance I had to beg Grant to hear my heart, I had to really make it count. Planting my palms on his cheeks, I pulled his face closer until our foreheads touched. "I don't know how to *live* without you. What am I going to do? Please. I'm begging you not to leave me. I'd rather die together than watch you leave and surely die apart."

When I pulled back to meet his beautiful blue stare, maybe for the last time ever, tears scorched hot tracks down my cheeks.

And now, Grant had matching tear streaks on his cheeks, too. "Stop. You stop right now," he said in a low, husky voice. "I told you what you have to do. Do you remember?"

"Please don't do this to me," I answered instead and wrapped my fingers around his forearm in a desperate grip. "Grant, please."

"Rio."

"Please."

In a flash, everything changed about Grant's demeanor. The set of his shoulders, the stiffness in his spine, even the light sky in his eyes darkened to a deep navy. When he spoke, the unmistakable Dominant tone vibrated through my entire body, and where goose bumps didn't prickle, little hairs stood on end.

He leveled his question one last time. "Do you remember what I told you?"

"Let's go, Twombley. Now." One of the kidnappers barked the command from his position near the door while another jabbed the barrel of his gun in the small of Grant's back.

"I love you, Blaze. Be brave for me." Grant kissed the top of my head and quickly moved out of my octopus arms' reach.

"Grant, please," I moaned just as I crumpled to the floor. I couldn't bear to watch him go.

"Get your fucking hands off me. I can walk myself," I heard Grant growl to one of his captors as they shoved him down the narrow passageway outside our door.

And stole him from me.

"Well, we don't want you getting any funny ideas," the leader's gravelly voice responded.

Soon, footsteps could be heard on the deck above our stateroom, and I scrambled into action. Grant told me to call Elijah or Sebastian as soon as he left, and I wouldn't let him down. I would do everything in my power to save him. Maybe Elijah could track Grant's phone as long as the thugs didn't take it from him. Hopefully he'd had a chance to stash it in an inconspicuous place.

Deep, throaty engines roared to life in the distance, and I scrambled to look out the bulkhead portholes in our cabin to see if I could catch a glimpse of their craft. Unfortunately, the crazy events that had just taken place had completely disoriented me on the time of day. No surprise, then, when I looked outside and saw nothing but pitch-black water and the star-filled sky. A quick glance at the clock on the bedside table informed me it was only 4:27 a.m. Now, the sliver of moon deep on the horizon made perfect sense.

At least something did.

I forced myself to stumble into the hallway, needing the mental clarity to form words.

"H-Help." Right now it was only one word, pathetic and raw and hoarse.

"Help!" Better, but not good enough.

I waited until reaching the deck to try for another, but it wouldn't be necessary. I stopped in my tracks, confronting five stares that likely matched mine for shell-shocked intent. I almost screamed, thinking our invaders had left behind a sweep team to take care of the crew and me permanently, but

I stopped short once I recognized all five of the faces.

And suddenly, horrifyingly, realized there should have been six.

I wasn't the only one. Leila, a member of the galley crew, shuffled forward like a refugee after a mortar attack. Like everyone else, she was dressed in a T-shirt and light pajama pants. There were still pillow lines across her cinnamon-colored cheeks.

"Harry?" she blurted from quivering lips. "Is he . . . with you, Ms. Gibson?"

Rio. My name is Rio, goddammit!

It was a scream in my mind, but she didn't deserve matching treatment from me, especially as her chin wobbled and tears welled in her huge amber gaze. My face must've become a billboard for the truth, and it was too late to pull it back.

"Those bastards must've taken him too. I'm sorry, you guys. I'm just so—"

I gritted back the rest of it. I couldn't keep following this tangent of despair. It wouldn't lead to good places. Or maybe that was up for interpretation. Because just a hallway away, nestled in an interior pocket of my handbag, was an emergency book of matches. And shit, would I qualify this as an emergency. I envisioned the perfect little square now. It was smooth and laminated, branded with a bright red-and-yellow logo of a Seal Beach auto repair place. While having service done on Kendall last month, I saw those little life preservers near the checkout register. I'd felt more relief about those fucking matches than I had about getting my car fixed.

No. *No.*

Grant needed me more than I needed that fix.

"Pardon?"

Shit. Leila's dulcet accent was laced with enough confusion to justify that I'd spilled my crazy tea aloud. But not so crazy, if I chose to focus on the part of it that mattered. And right now, I had to fucking focus.

"He needs me." I swung my newly determined stare around at all of them. "He needs all of us. They both do." Noticing how my rushed words seemed to jolt all of them out of a collective daze, I scraped together slivers of courage and molded them into a bolder tone. "Has anyone gotten on the radio yet? Isn't there some kind of an emergency hail we can start sending out? What?" The self-interruption was my choice, blurted as soon as I locked stares with Leila again. "What is it?" I charged, certain she'd start wringing her hands any moment.

"The radio," she muttered. "It's . . ."

"It's what?"

"Broken," one of the deckhands supplied. "That's probably where they found Harry and—"

Leila's pained sob sent him into grimacing silence. In one form or another, we all joined him.

"Okay, everyone take a minute and breathe," I said brusquely, scrounging deep for a part of my psyche that hadn't seen exercise in a while. It was my get-shit-done bravado, usually yanked out for occasions like making potato salad when the potatoes were delivered late, or a last-minute anniversary party for fifty, or an awards night after party with a thousand of Hollywood's elite in the next room. But there was no next room here. And unless I pulled my shit together and turned everyone's tears into fuel, there'd be no help on the way for the man I loved.

ANGEL PAYNE & VICTORIA BLUE

"I'm going to the upper deck to see if I can get a cell signal. Mr. Twombley has a few friends in high places."

When the captain arrived on deck, nobody wasted any more time, so neither did I. After sprinting my way up to the flybridge, I rasped a fervent prayer before unlocking my phone again. I ended that prayer with tearful gratitude. Three bars. I'd take it. I had to.

Fortunately, Shark Enterprises' main switchboard number was saved in my phone. On the rare occasion Abstract was running late with deliveries to the offices, it was handy for fast dialing. I ignored the tremble of my finger as I selected the number now.

"Hello. Thank you for calling Shark Enterprises International. Our normal business hours are eight a.m. to six p.m. Pacific Time, but your call is very important to us. To access our company voice mail directory, please select—"

Suppressing a curse, I jabbed at the zero. No way in hell was there nobody in that building, even at this hour of the day.

"You have reached the Shark Enterprises main line. Our offices are currently closed but will reopen at eight o'clock a.m. Pacific Time. If you need to reach someone right away—"

Another stab at the zero. I'd talk to someone in person at that damn building, even if I had to call LAFD and have them break the doors in.

After five rings, my anxiety mounted. I was preparing to punch at the zero again, when there was crackling on the line. Not electronic, though. It sounded more like a starving person digging into a bag of chips.

"Hello?" I croaked. "Hello, is someone—"

"Shark Enterprises, security desk," a bored voice drawled.

"Hi," I blurted. "Hi. Sorry. Thank you for picking up." I

meant it so completely, I nearly choked on it. "Is this Shark Enterprises?"

"Ma'am, I just said that."

"Right. You did. Please, I need your help. I really, really need your help. I need to talk to somebody. I need to talk to them now."

I nearly strung it together as one sentence, though my punctuation could've been the hand I pounded at my temple. The throbbing was back in my brain, beckoning me back to the blessed darkness behind my eyelids. I fought it with every strength I had—which wasn't much.

"The offices are closed right now, ma'am, but I can patch you through to the voice mail—"

"No! No voice mail, please! I'm on a boat in the middle of the Pacific, and this is an emergency."

"Ah. I'll patch you through to maritime operations."

"I don't need them."

"I beg your pardon, ma'am, but if you're on a vessel and this matter is urgent, then you need—"

"Elijah Banks." I released a breath, wanting to leap in joy that the name had finally slammed my brain. "I—I think he's on Mr. Shark's personal team in some capacity."

"Oh. Then you do need the voice mail dir—"

"No! I fucking need Elijah Banks, on this line, right now!" I yearned to punch a wall, but there was only the damn sky and a hopelessly empty horizon. How the hell had those bastards gotten away so far, so fast? "Please. I'm begging you. This really is an emergency. Lives are stake! You must have Mr. Banks's direct number there. Can you put down the Doritos for one second and dial it?"

I was going to regret the crack. Damn it, I already did. The guy's affronted grunt told me as much.

But just as I braced myself for an ear full of dial tone, there was a new sound on the other end of the line. An angry, incessant buzz. A hail that had Doritos king shifting uncomfortably in his chair—cue the squeaky support gears— before huffing even louder at me.

"Hold please," he mumbled.

I held. For my dear life. For Grant's too.

The line reengaged with an odd collection of clumsy clicks. Once more I battled the despair of a disconnection, which was surely coming any second. Until . . .

"Who the fuck is this?"

I startled. Not my snack-loving friend. The voice was a vaguely recognizable snarl but not Shark himself. I'd recognize that arrogant ass's baritone anytime.

"Who is this?" I retorted.

At first, there was only a violent snag of breath. A long, questioning pause. At last he ventured, "Rio? Is this you?"

I stopped pacing, though I was frazzled and punchy and desperate enough to claw a hand at my hairline again. "Who wants to know?"

"Rio. Thank God."

He didn't charge at that flank again. "Where are you?" he demanded instead. "Are you with Twombley? What's the trouble?"

My heart stuttered as I squeezed my eyes shut, telling myself it wasn't time for panic yet. *Not. Yet.* I still had to find the strength to be brave because I promised I would be brave. I had to suck up the air for words and be brave.

"No. I'm not with him. He's . . . not here."

"Okay." There was a lot of rustling, like papers being

sorted. His voice jostled as if he were doing five things at once. "I suspected as much."

"You did?" I dropped my hand. My head jerked up. "How—"

"I got his text. Well, part of it."

"His what?" My gaze bugged. My spirit soared. "A text?" Relief buckled my knees. I crumpled to the deck, no longer dreaming of torching it. "He did manage to hide his phone. If those assholes don't find it, we can track—"

"Whoa. Assholes?" he interjected. "What assholes? Who the fuck has his phone?"

I huffed. "But you said you got his text."

"We have a code. Bas, him, and me. Three exclamation points. Eight minutes ago, I only received two."

My knees went weak again—for a much different reason. "Fuck," I croaked. Then whispered, "Elijah, you have to help him . . ."

"Rio. Hey. Rio!" He stressed it like I'd become hearing impaired. With the chaos and dread taking over my senses, that was likely the truth. "Stay with me, girl. I'm going to help him. Fuck, I'm going to call in every favor from every resource I've got to do it, but I need a plan. To have that, I need details. As many of them as you can give me. Go back to the start, and don't leave anything out."

★ ★ ★

I had no idea how I made it through that ordeal, especially the parts about watching Grant get led away by those disgusting creeps. Worse than that was having to tell Elijah I didn't have a single detail about their getaway vessel. Not even stored in the recesses of my memory. His cavalcade of reassurances, that they likely had something nondescript and fast on purpose, provided scant comfort.

Correction. They were no consolation at all.

Which meant that now, as the sun breached the horizon, I was beyond drained. Past consolable. And plummeting into my inner danger zone.

I trudged back to the stateroom—purposely bypassing my purse on the desk in favor of a fall into bed. I needed a distraction. Lots of it. I'd need it for the next thirty-six hours at least, until we docked in Marina del Rey. Though Elijah had offered to send a helicopter for me, I'd turned him down. That would be one less machine dedicated to the hunt for Grant and Harry.

The first leg of my journey back to real mental health.

The baby steps I wasn't expecting to make on my own.

Fuck. *Fuck.*

I figured the day ahead would go much better if I had some sleep behind me. Getting beneath the covers flooded me with Grant's distinct smell, and I immediately went to pieces as the rich woodsy notes flooded my senses.

After three hours of tossing and turning atop the covers, all I had to show for my diligent efforts were a frightful case of bedhead, seriously jangled nerves, hideously swollen eyes, and a defined plan to discreetly pack all the bedsheets before I disembarked in Los Angeles. Hey, desperate times called for desperate measures—and I was nothing if not desperate.

My decision kicked off several frantic inspections of our cabin, making sure I hadn't left a single thing of his behind. As more tears threatened, I even snatched the bath towel Grant had last used, folded the white rectangle as if it were the

Pope's vestments, and placed it in my suitcase as well. I never imagined I'd be packing with a broken heart like this twice in one lifetime.

How was this fair? At fucking all?

Each bitter query carried the weight of a thousand more tears, dissolving the last thin threads of my self-control. "Damn it!" I muttered, hating my weakness as I swiped at my cheeks.

I had to contain this bullshit again. At this rate, I wouldn't survive until today's sunset, let alone until LA.

"Okay, okay," I ordered in a whisper, finally convincing myself that if I lit just one or two matches and let them burn themselves out in the shower, there'd be no harm. No one would know. No one had to. Most importantly, no one would be in danger.

I got everything I needed for my last shower on board this vessel, as well as the three matches that I would burn. But when it was over, I didn't feel any better. In fact, I felt worse. I'd let myself down. More terribly, I'd let down a lot of important people—including the one who'd become so important and special to me. Grant was likely tied up in some dank cargo hold, wondering if he'd ever see the light of day again, and I was over here breaking the most important promise I'd ever made to him. Of course, he would never know I had. Nobody would. But I was ashamed to the core of my being, and I was the one who would have to live with that.

Late afternoon the next day, we slowly glided into the harbor at Marina del Rey. I stood on the yacht's main deck, certain I was about to crawl out of my skin, as we passed the first couple of basins and finally eased toward our assigned slip. Four dock masters stood with ropes in hand, awaiting our vessel's return. The captain guided the yacht in stern first, and while his care was to be admired, I was jumpy as hell.

Sleep had continued to be an elusive bitch for me last night, and the crew's weary faces around me conveyed they'd faced the same. The only creature who seemed to be getting any rest was Robert, who snoozed soundly in his carrier thanks to the mild sedative I'd put in his food this morning.

I filled the wait time by doing something useful. I hurried below to conduct one last check of the cabin Grant and I had shared for two glorious weeks.

Tears filled my eyes and then spilled down both cheeks while I spent several long minutes looking around the room, heatedly debating with myself.

Should I go or stay?

A simple decision from the outside, but not from within.

Part of me felt like leaving the room, let alone the boat, would be like already giving up on him. On us. On everything we'd shared during this journey. It felt like I was minimizing every promise we made. Erasing every forward step we'd taken together. There would be no history recorded to prove we did the work. There would be no evidence we put in the time. The hopes and dreams we told each other, the laughs we laughed— even the tears we cried in here—would all be gone.

Just like he was.

My tears came harder. Anguish choked me, making it difficult to breathe. "Damn it," I gritted beneath my breath. "Stop it!"

I refused to just give it all up. Not again. I already knew I wasn't good at moving on. I'd just had a harsh lesson from that textbook. I knew it didn't end well for a girl like me.

So I was choosing the only path that remained.

The resolve that made sense.

I had to help Elijah find him. This damsel in distress bit didn't suit me either. Just before Grant left with the pirates, I'd quietly promised him I'd be brave. I wasn't about to take it back. I would not become a sad, helpless victim.

I. Would. Not.

A soft knock on the cabin's newly fixed door startled me from my pep talk. I swiped my fingertips across my cheeks and blinked rapidly, hoping like hell I didn't look like too much of a basket case to whoever was here to say goodbye.

"Wh—" My voice came out sounding scratchy, not that I'd be fooling anyone about my bravery at this rate. After a hearty cough, I swung the panel wide. "Can I help you?"

"Mrs. Gibson? I'm—uh—um—here to carry your bags out." Christ, if this kid acted any more nervous, I would offer him some of Robert's kitty tranquilizer. "Also, someone is waiting for you dockside. A gentleman. Just thought you'd want to know."

"Thank you," I said quietly. "I'll be up in a few minutes."

Through flared nostrils, I sucked in one final, fortifying breath of the precious air I had shared with Grant. It was time to leave, but I couldn't bring myself to walk out the door. I wanted to throw myself on the floor and kick and scream and have a toddler-sized tantrum.

"Would you like me to wait, then?" the young deckhand asked. "The captain asked me to help you down the gangway if you needed it, ma'am."

"Not necessary." I forced a smile again. "But if you wouldn't mind telling the gentleman on the dock that I just needed a minute and am on my way . . ."

"Of course."

With a polite click, he shut the door again.

Seconds after that, I sank to my knees in the middle of the room.

"I can't... do this."

Only silence answered back. Not even Robert twitched, sound asleep in his portable bed.

"This wasn't part of the deal, Twombley. You told me you'd be here to help!"

More silence.

"Grant. Damn it! I can't do this. I can't!"

Silence.

Taunting me. Tempting me.

So maybe I'd called the fucker's bluff.

My hands trembled as I retrieved the smooth white matchbook from the hidden pocket inside my purse. Six dedicated soldiers still stood in my army. But that was all. Just six.

I rocked back on my heels, pulling my hair in desperation. Shit. Why was this so hard? Why did I keep fucking everything up? I knocked on the side of my head with the heel of my hand and instantly thought of Grant's anguished face every time I'd given in to one of my dark episodes. I never remembered much from any of those visits in the shadows of my psyche, but emerging from them brought agony I couldn't describe.

Grant had been there every time—with pain across his face that gutted me.

But maybe that's why he wasn't here now. Perhaps all of this was simply some elaborate setup to get rid of me. To be free of my fucked-to-shit drama.

"Enough!" I shouted aloud, battling another flood of self-loathing when Robert started and glowered out at me. "No," I muttered to myself. "Just no. Not now. Just get your shit together, okay? You aren't spinning out of control right now. You don't have time for this crap. Grant needs you, so get your ass off this boat and get home."

At least I knew when I left this room, all I had to do was survive a straight shot down the freeway to my house. No, wait. Maybe I could just go to Grant's downtown condo. He'd shared the key with me one day after stating the obvious: it was much closer to the prep kitchen. But right now, I was thinking more about law enforcement offices, local and international, than the kitchen. I had no idea who had jurisdiction over an event like this, in waters hundreds of miles off the coast, but I'd be much more readily available for anyone and everyone who needed my help. The only issue would be not having Kendall. Christ. Where was my car? What made me think I could help save the man I loved from fucking pirates when I couldn't even keep track of a Fiat?

Elijah swept me into his embrace the moment I reached the bottom of the angled plank.

"Thank you for coming. I didn't know who else to call."

"Don't be ridiculous. I wouldn't be anywhere else," Elijah said before kissing both my cheeks. "Try to keep your voice down while we're here though. You never know who may be feeding the press. So far, we've managed to keep it out of the media. Okay?" He made his greeting look so effortless when it was actually an opportunity to issue his advice about keeping our voices low.

"Right. Of course." I nodded and then looked around with open curiosity. I wasn't sure if Sebastian had come or if he was waiting to debrief at home behind closed doors. "For some reason, I expected Shark to be here with you."

He looked boyish when he shrugged with more swagger

than should be legal for one person. "Sorry to disappoint you."

"You know what I meant," I clarified. "But let's get to the more important point." I curled a taut hand around his forearm. "Tell me right now. Have you made any headway with finding him? Please, Elijah, I need some hope to hold on to."

The look on my face had to be pitiful by the time I got the statement out, but there was nothing I could do to change it. Nothing I cared to do either. I needed the information more than I needed my next breath. If he thought I was going to delay the question as a breezy conversation filler once we hit the 405, he was thoroughly mistaken.

But Elijah came back with an answer—okay, a nonanswer—just as telling.

Grant's handsome friend, appearing just as pleasant as the moment before, motioned to the bags on the ground around us. "Is this everything?"

Either the guy didn't have a shred of an update to relay, or a change of subject was his desperate ploy to save himself from having to comfort a woman on the verge of tears. Either way, I got the hint. After hitching my big-girl panties a little higher, I turned in a full circle to take in all the luggage. Grant had left behind one bag, along with another that he'd originally packed for me. In a third suitcase were the souvenirs and gifts we had picked up in Hawaii. I held Robert's carrier in one hand, but where was my handbag?

"Crap," I groused, realizing I hadn't grabbed it on my way out. "Can you load this stuff in the car while I go back for my handbag?"

"Sure. I'll pull right up to the loading zone, by that white van."

I hurried back up the gangway and then aboard the boat.

But just a few steps on deck, and they were already faltering. My limbs were shaky and mushy. I stopped completely, struggling just to get in air.

Already, I knew the disgusting reason why.

I couldn't do it. I couldn't leave this yacht and the life-changing events that had occurred on it. I thought I'd be able to, but I couldn't. This was worse than mere nerves. I was in the throes of an anxiety attack. It wasn't like saying goodbye to the East Coast, not knowing what waited for me out here. It wasn't even like the day Abbi and I signed the lease on the bigger kitchen space in Inglewood. Neither of those occasions came with this terrible feeling that if I drove away from this yacht with Elijah, I wouldn't be leaving just the boat behind.

I would never see Grant again.

The dread persisted as I forced my feet deeper into the vessel. My hand trembled as I tried the knob to our cabin. To my joy, it was still unlocked. The cleaning crew was making their way around the boat but hadn't come by our room yet, thank God.

I slipped inside, treasuring the close comfort of the familiar space, before coming to an irrefutable decision. The only option left.

I had to destroy the entire yacht.

"Yes," I declared softly. "Perfect."

I'd rarely been more certain of a course in my entire life. It made overriding sense. If the boat were gone, I wouldn't actually be leaving it behind, and I wouldn't be leaving Grant behind.

And he would come back to me.

I raced around the room now, snatching up all the paper items I could find. Stationery from different marinas we visited, an old paperback mystery novel from the nightstand drawer, and a plain yellow notepad from an office supply store. On Grant's side of the bed, there were a few days' worth of *Wall Street Journals* and another mystery novel by the same author. I vowed to send the guy a check, feeling so guilty for what was about to happen to two of his books.

At once, I took it all to the bathroom.

I opened the cabinet under the sink and knelt before it. There was no way I could do all the necessary damage by starting something in the sink. Undoubtedly a smoke detector would go off and some do-gooder would rush in to save the day, fire extinguisher in hand. I rolled my eyes at the thought, even though I was alone, and assessed the space beneath the sink. This would have to be my spot.

Assembling the pyre was one of my favorite parts of starting a blaze. It was thrilling and ritualistic—ancient and celebratory. To an outsider, a fire was just destruction, vandalism, or danger. But to me, it was a creation of beauty and expression. Entire civilizations had been both controlled and destroyed by fire. The power in that notion was so intoxicating and irresistible it gave me chills just thinking about it.

I gave my head a little shake and looked down at my white matchbook. My heartbeat quickened. My blood warmed. No more shame now. Only anticipation and excitement. The matchsticks were lined up so neatly, reminding me of little baseball players waiting in the dugout for their turn to play.

"Batter up," an imaginary umpire called, and a flurry of butterflies dominated my stomach. My team had to win, and we were in the home stretch . . .

Until my cell phone buzzed in my back pocket.

I quickly looked at the screen. It was a text from Elijah,

wondering what was taking so long.

Goddammit. Fucking buzzkill.

I tapped a quick reply that one of the crew members was subjecting me to a chatty farewell. A smile breached my lips when realizing the lie actually gave me the excuse I needed. One last sentence to assure him I'd be out as soon as possible, before stuffing my phone back in my pocket. Definitely didn't want to leave anything behind when I hurried out of here.

But now I was pissed at my sulfur-headed team. Nobody was connecting so far, and I didn't have all damn day. Another player stepped up to bat. He had to deliver; otherwise there would be singed paper and other evidence under the sink in our cabin. The vessel's owner would want answers.

I struck the little redhead on the flint strip. A surge of satisfying power hit my bloodstream as I watched it flare to life. The air inside the cabin was still, so the infant flame grew straight up, a miniature torch.

Calmly, I placed the fire in the middle of the debris and lightly fanned oxygen toward the flame.

"Ahh." I exhaled a sigh of relief. "That's what I needed two batters ago."

I struck another match, letting it flare. Already I could see the perfect spot to set it, and I crouched low to ensure I was getting it right now. *Yes, yes. Grow for me now. Live for me . . .*

A sound sliced into my transfixed high. A completely unmistakable sound. It made me freeze in place.

Was that . . . a baby?

What the hell?

I remained that way for two more seconds, listening intently.

Shit. Maybe I really was going insane.

I sat there and contemplated the issue for another long second. Another. During my existential inquiry—because apparently, the fate of nations really did rest on whether I was officially insane or not—the match burned onto its cardboard container and reached my fingertips. The heat took a few seconds to register in my jumbled brain, so when I instinctively shook my hand from the burn, the whole flame got snuffed out.

Mother. Fucker.

My only hope of saving Grant—snuffed out.

"Rio?" a familiar voice said. "Oh no, sister. What are you doing?"

"Abbi?"

I rubbed my eyes because I had to be hallucinating. But when I looked up, my judgmental sister-in-law was indeed standing in the bathroom doorway—and she had a little blue bundle cradled in her arms. My gaze flashed from hers to the swaddle and then to hers again. She was holding Kaisan. My nephew. Part of Sean's legacy.

"Rio," Abbigail gasped. "Don't do it."

CONTINUE READING
THE SHARK'S EDGE SERIES

Coming Soon!

ALSO BY
ANGEL PAYNE & VICTORIA BLUE

Shark's Edge Series:
Shark's Edge
Shark's Pride
Shark's Rise
Grant's Heat
Grant's Flame
Grant's Blaze

Secrets of Stone Series:
No Prince Charming
No More Masquerade
No Perfect Princess
No Magic Moment
No Lucky Number
No Simple Sacrifice
No Broken Bond
No White Knight
No Longer Lost

ALSO BY ANGEL PAYNE

The Blood of Zeus Series:
(with Meredith Wild)
Blood of Zeus
Heart of Fire
Fate of Storms

The Bolt Saga:
Bolt
Ignite
Pulse
Fuse
Surge
Light

Misadventures:
Misadventures with a Time Traveler

Honor Bound:
Saved
Cuffed
Seduced
Wild
Wet
Hot
Masked
Mastered
Conquered
Ruled

Cimarron Series:
Into His Dark
Into His Command
Into Her Fantasies

Temptation Court:
Naughty Little Gift
Pretty Perfect Toy
Bold Beautiful Love

Suited for Sin:
Sing
Sigh
Submit

Lords of Sin:
Trade Winds
Promised Touch
Redemption
A Fire in Heaven
Surrender to the Dawn

ALSO BY VICTORIA BLUE

Misadventures:
Misadventures with a Book Boyfriend
Misadventures at City Hall

**For a full list of Angel's & Victoria's other titles,
visit them at AngelPayne.com & VictoriaBlue.com**

ACKNOWLEDGMENTS

A world of thanks to so many wonderful people who help us with all the things, each and every day!

Our families, who are there through it all. Thank you, Team Blue and Team Payne!

Our assistants and cheering squads: Megan Ashley, Amy Bourne, Martha Frantz, and Kika Medina.

The entire crew at Waterhouse Press: you are a Dream Team beyond compare!

The amazing readers in Victoria's Book Secrets and Payne Passion: we love you guys so much!

ABOUT ANGEL PAYNE

USA Today bestselling romance author Angel Payne loves to focus on high-heat romance starring memorable alpha men and the women who love them. She has numerous book series to her credit, including the action-packed Bolt Saga and Honor Bound series, Secrets of Stone series (with Victoria Blue), the intertwined Cimarron and Temptation Court series, the Suited for Sin series, and the Lords of Sin historicals, as well as several standalone titles.

Angel is a native Southern Californian, leading to her love of being in the outdoors, where she often reads and writes. She still lives in Southern California with her soul-mate husband and beautiful daughter, to whom she is a proud cosplay/culture con mom. Her passions also include whisky tasting, shoe shopping, and travel.

Visit her at AngelPayne.com

ABOUT VICTORIA BLUE

International bestselling author Victoria Blue lives in her own portion of the galaxy known as Southern California. There, she finds the love and life-sustaining power of one amazing sun, two unique and awe-inspiring planets, and four indifferent yet comforting moons. Life is fantastic and challenging and every day brings new adventures to be discovered. She looks forward to seeing what's next!

Visit her at VictoriaBlue.com

ALSO FROM
ANGEL PAYNE & VICTORIA BLUE

THE SECRETS OF STONE SERIES

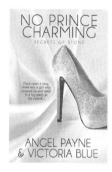

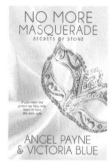

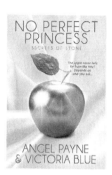

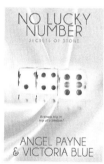

ALSO FROM
ANGEL PAYNE

THE BOLT SAGA

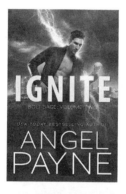

ALSO FROM
WATERHOUSE PRESS

IN THE MISADVENTURES SERIES